PEAS & HAMBONE

D1497428

PEAS & HAMBONE

SAVE US ALL

WRITTEN BY
TODD NICHOLS

ILLUSTRATED BY
CHRIS CAVATORTA

SecretSquirrel Books

This is a work of fiction. Names, characters, places, and incidents are either products of the author's imagination or, if real, are used fictitiously.

Copyright © 2017 by Todd Nichols

All rights reserved. No part of this book may be reproduced, transmitted, or stored in any information retrieval system in any form or by any means, graphic, electronic, or mechanical, including photocopying, taping, and recording, without prior written permission from the publisher.

Second edition 2018

Library of Congress Card Number pending
ISBN 978-0-6929-3832-4

This book was typeset in Raleway.
The illustrations were done in Pen and ink.

Secret Squirrel Books
Bedford, Massachusetts

VISIT WWW.PEASANDHAMBONE.COM
FOR DOWNLOADS, ACTIVITIES AND MORE!

Peas and Hambone say: **READ, READ, READ!**

Read books, more books, backs of cereal boxes, magazines, labels on cans, comics, graphic novels, tubes of toothpaste, graffiti, directions, instruction booklets, your best friend's mind.

Read everything you can get your hands on.

(But, no, don't read your annoying little sister's diary. Unless you get her permission, of course.)

Read every day.

Read to learn, for fun, to laugh, to cry, to be inspired, to help you fall asleep at night, to grow ideas, to change the world.

Always be reading.

Do it today.

CHAPTER ONE

LEMON SNOW CONE, ANYONE?

My name is Peter.

But you can call me Peas. That's P-E-A-S. Like the vegetable. Not like the other kind, the one with the two e's that's not a vegetable at all. Has nothing to do with little green spheres or giant green...well, giants. Ho—ho—ho.

No.

The one with the two e's has to do with a certain bodily function we all do, but it's not like I want

to spell it out for you.

Here's a clue: it has to do with yellow streams and "Don't eat the yellow snow!"

Which is gross, but I've seen a kid do it.

I'm thinking about the time Joey Zabroski convinced Marcus Winkleman that the yellow snow tasted like a lemon snow cone—so he ate it. Gobbled it all down and even said he liked the tangy taste. If you can believe it.

Marcus isn't that bright. He says it's because his older sister dropped him on his head when he was a baby. But I don't think that's the reason. I think it's because of all the yellow snow he's eaten in his life. It can't be good for brain functioning.

So back to what I'm telling you.

Peas is my nickname. And before you start in on how ridiculous that nickname is, let me just say that I agree with you. It's a ridiculous nickname. I don't know why my dad started calling me that. Well, I have a clue. He's always saying me and him are like "two peas in a pod." I guess that's where he got it from.

So why am I telling you this?

Why am I opening myself up to embarrassment and potential ridicule by letting millions of people know my ridiculous nickname?

I'm telling you this so you can see for yourself what kind of kid I am.

I'm honest. Straight out, I'm going to tell you the truth, no matter the cost to me or my reputation.

This is important. It's important because of what I'm going to tell you next.

I have a dog. His name is Hambone.

3

I know. Not earth-shattering news. But here's the earth-shattering part: the thing about Hambone is that he's not only a dog— he's also a kid. Just like me. Whenever he wants, he can walk on two legs and talk and do everything any kid can do.

Impossible, you say? I thought so at first too. (*I mean, it's not like I've been eating yellow snow all my life.*)

But it is possible. But only when Hambone is with me.

He doesn't do it when other people are around.

I didn't know this at first. So I told my family that Hambone is not a dog but a kid even though he doesn't look like a kid, he looks like a dog.

Of course, that didn't go over real well.

My mom and dad both laughed and

4

said I was crazy.

And I guess it's a good thing I'm an only child. I'd hate to think what a brother or sister would have said. Probably that I was loco, nuts, cuckoo for Cocoa Puffs. That I should be wrapped tight in a straightjacket and taken to the loony bin. Which sounds like a fun place. Isn't that where they keep all the Looney Tunes characters like Bugs Bunny and Elmer Fudd? That would be a pretty cool place to go.

But what was I saying?

Oh, yeah. My mom and dad both think I'm crazy.

I told Hambone this. He laughed. He said that I should let them think that. He said that whenever anybody sees us together, he'll make sure to go back to being a dog doing dog stuff. So nobody will ever know the truth. It will be our little secret, he said.

Well, now it's ours and yours.

But you have to swear not to tell anybody else.

If you do that, we're cool.

Besides, if you tell people, they're going to think you're crazy.

And you don't want that.

You might wind up in the loony bin.

So we're cool?

Good.

Because what I really want to start telling you about is the time me and

6

Hambone had to stop Evil Doctor Crazy Gorilla from taking over the world. His plan was to create an army of zombie gorillas dead set on eating the flesh of every human on the face of the planet until there weren't any humans left. Only zombie gorillas.

And his plan would have worked, too, if it weren't for me and Hambone.

We saved the human race.

But I'm getting ahead of myself.

Before we saved the human race, we went to the zoo.

And that's where it all started.

CHAPTER TWO

TICKETS? WE DON'T NEED NO STINKIN' TICKETS!

I'm standing in front of Hambone, trying to block any of the zoo workers from seeing what he's doing.

Which is digging a hole underneath the fence that surrounds the zoo. I can hear Hambone cursing to himself as he digs.

Somebody filled in the hole he started yesterday. So now he has to start all over again.

"If I find out who did this, they're gonna be sorry," he says. "Maybe leave a nice little calling card on the roof of their car, if you know what I'm saying."

"Maybe they're on to us," I say.

Hambone sniffs. "Doubt it," he says. "But if you think so, you'd better keep a good lookout."

I keep a good lookout.

Out of the corner of my eye, I see something moving. A car is pulling into the zoo's parking lot.

"Pssst," I say over my shoulder. "Ixnay on the iggingday."

"How about ixnay on the pssstay?" says Hambone, continuing to dig.

The car comes closer to where we are. It stops.

This isn't good.

I'll tell you what else isn't good. The people in the car stare right at me. They know! They know!!

"Let's get out of here," I say.

"What are you talking about?" says Hambone. "I just started."

"But they're on to us."

"Who?"

I point to the...um, where did it go? I swear the car was here a second ago. Oh, there it is. It's heading out of the parking lot

10

and getting back on the road.

False alarm.

Phew!

But still. What if another car pulls into the parking lot? Not somebody who's lost, but somebody who's coming to the zoo. The zoo doesn't open for another hour, but what's to stop some family from getting here a little early trying to be first in line?

"Why don't we just wait for the zoo to open like everybody else?" I say.

"Are you kidding me?" says Hambone. "I'm not paying seven dollars to look at a bunch of dumb animals. If I wanted to do that, I'd just look in the mirror. Save the seven bucks."

He stops digging and thinks about what he just said. "That didn't come out right. But you know what I mean. Pay like

//

everybody else? Where's the fun in that?"

I look down at the hole I'm going to have to crawl through.

"This is fun?" I say.

"The fun is in doing something dangerous—something that will get us into trouble if we get caught," says Hambone. "That's the juice. The jazz. What makes us alive. And what separates us from those dummies in their cages." He nods his head in the direction of the zoo's entrance.

I guess now is as good a time as any to tell you that Hambone lives life on the edge. And since I'm always with him—he's my best friend—I end up right there on the edge too.

Like now.

Hambone stands up.

"OK," he says, wiping the dirt off his

paws. "That should be good enough. See if you can fit through."

I get down on my stomach and begin to army-crawl under the fence. I fit my head through just fine, but then the collar of my shirt gets snagged on a piece of wire jutting out.

I carefully rock back and forth to try and get unsnagged.

It doesn't work. All it does is snag me more. And now I can feel the piece of wire against my skin. It feels like the long fingernail of Big Boy Bob, from *Crazy Clowns at the Circus.*

I love that movie. So does Hambone. But we love all kinds of movies. I guess you could say we're movie fanatics. We love movies so much we sometimes talk to each other using lines from our favorite ones. It's kind of our thing.

(Dear Reader, You may not know when we are doing it so we have marked the lines with a 🎬 *emoji. Check out the guide at the end of this book if you want to know what movie they come from. Sincerely, Peas and Hambone.)*

I stay perfectly still.

If I make a sudden move, Big Boy Bob's fingernail...um, I mean, the piece of wire will slice into my flesh. Maybe hit an artery.

Oh, the horror.

Of course, that's not going to actually happen. But what if it did? Hambone doesn't have any fingers to plug up my artery. And if he runs for help, nobody will believe him. He's not Lassie, you know.

"I could use a little help here," I say.

14

Hambone puts his foot on my butt.

"What are you doing?" I say. "Are you crazy? Don't you see that wire I'm caught on? Do you want it to slice me open?"

"Frankly, Peas, I don't give a dump," says Hambone.

I think he's joking.

I hope he's joking.

With his foot still on my butt, Hambone shoves me as hard as he can. I'm propelled through the hole and into the zoo. In the process, the wire tears a hole in my shirt but doesn't do any damage to my flesh. I'm lucky.

"What were you thinking?" I say.

"Don't be such a baby," says Hambone, crawling under the fence. "There's not a scratch on you."

"But there could have been."

"But there's not. So let's go."

Boy, some best friend.

Chapter 3

Revenge-Fu

We walk past the signpost pointing to the reptiles.

We walk past the signpost pointing to the Mexican gray wolf.

We walk past the signpost pointing to the peacock place.

This zoo has everything.

If I didn't know where we were going, I'd be lost.

But I know where we're going.

Straight to the gorillas.

I follow Hambone down a path that has all these trees on either side so it looks like we're walking through a forest. Once we get to the end, the path opens up into a clearing. That's where all the gorillas do their gorilla stuff.

"Boy, do I hate this place," says Hambone.

It's true. Hambone hates everything gorilla. In fact, he says he has a special kind of hate for them. *(I think it stems from some childhood trauma involving the movie King Gorilla.)*

So why are we going to the Gorilla Kingdom?

Revenge!

Last summer one of the gorillas picked up some dirt and threw it at Hambone. Not on purpose. At least, I thought it was all very innocent like. But Hambone didn't see it that way. He took it personally. As if the gorilla had done it on purpose because he knew how much Hambone hates gorillas. And ever since that day, he swore he'd get even.

"Do you know what I'm going to do to that gorilla when I see him again?" says Hambone, stopping at the moat at the edge of the clearing.

(I think it's funny that it's called a moat. Because when you think of moats, you usually think of them surrounding castles, not gorillas.)

"No," I say. "What are you going to do to that gorilla?"

"Allow me to enlighten you," he says. "I'm going to unleash the power of Dog Fu on him."

"Not the ancient martial art known as Dog Fu," I gasp.

"That's right," says Hambone, striking a Dog Fu pose. "You mess with me, you get the paws."

(Speaking of Dog Fu, Hambone once unleashed it on this little poodle who tried to sniff his butt. I think the poodle was just saying hello. Hambone didn't agree. Let's just say he didn't say "Hi" back.)

Hambone walks right up to the edge of the moat.

He looks around the clearing at all the gorillas, trying to figure out which one is the one he wants.

"It's hard with them all being asleep," he says.

"Maybe we should come back later," I say.

Hambone ignores me. "Is that the one?" he says, pointing to a gorilla asleep on top of a fallen tree.

"I don't know," I say. "It could be."

"Here, gorilla, gorilla. Here, gorilla," says Hambone.

The gorilla doesn't move.

Hambone leans over the moat and screams, "Wake up you big, dumb gorilla!

It's go time."

"I don't think screaming at him is going to work," I say.

"Oh, yeah," he says. "Well, if he doesn't wake up soon, I'll tell you what's going to work: me swimming across this moat and unleashing some Dog Fu on him."

I can tell Hambone means business.

Which makes me think: Uh-oh. This isn't going to end well.

CHAPTER FOUR

YOU SAY BALLERINA,
I SAY MAD SCIENTIST

Hambone takes off his collar.

"Here," he says, handing it to me. "Hold this. I don't want it to get wet."

"What are you doing?" I say.

"Just what I said I was going to do, If that gorilla thinks I'm playing around, he's sadly mistaken."

"You're seriously going to swim over there? How? Doggie paddle?"

"Very funny."

Hambone gets set to dive in.

"Wait a second," I say. "Look over there."

I'm pointing to this guy who has suddenly appeared out of nowhere.

"What about him?" says Hambone.

"Who is he?"

"He's not a big, dumb gorilla. So I don't care."

"Well, whoever he is, he sure is weird looking."

And when I say weird looking, I mean weird looking. His hair is a bunch of silvery-white strands. It looks as if somebody plopped a handful of tinsel on top of his head. He's wearing green-tinted sunglasses, a red bow tie, black gloves that go all the way up to his shoulder, a white lab coat that

goes all the way down to his knees, and yellow sneakers.

I start laughing.

"What's so funny?" says Hambone.

"I was just thinking about all those really bad science-fiction movies we've seen," I say. "And how there's always this crazy mad-scientist guy in them. That's what this weird-looking guy reminds me of."

"Mad scientist? You think he's a mad scientist?"

"If he is, he needs a name. All the ones in the movies I've seen have funny-sounding names. Like Evil Doctor Baron Von Frickenstein. Or Evil Doctor Siegfried Van Der Dorff. I think I shall call this weird-looking guy Evil Doctor Crazy Gorilla."

"That's pretty good," says Hambone.

Just then, Evil Doctor Crazy Gorilla looks over in our direction.

"Quick," I say, diving behind a trash barrel. "Before he sees us."

I hear Hambone sigh.

"What are you doing?" he says, walking over to me.

I look up at him. "Obviously I'm ducking for cover."

"Seriously?" he says. "He wasn't even looking at us."

"It sure looked like he was. And who knows what Evil Doctor Crazy Gorilla might do if he knows we are watching him?"

Hambone sniffs. "Get up," he says. "Nothing is going to happen."

"How can you be so sure?" I say.

"Because he's not a mad scientist. I bet he's just some guy who sleeps in the zoo. He's harmless."

"Says you. But what if he really is a mad scientist?"

"What if he's really a ballerina? Or a magical being from the fairy planet Tinkerdust?"

"You know, sarcasm doesn't become you."

"Fine. But why don't we just take it down a notch. See what this guy is up to before jumping to any conclusions."

"OK," I say, getting up from behind the trash barrel. "But you should be warned. If he really is a mad scientist, they don't take kindly to people messing with their evil plans. I can tell you that."

"Look at me; I'm shaking," he says.

I look at him.

He's not shaking.

"Don't say I didn't warn you," I say.

We watch as Evil Doctor Crazy Gorilla goes over to the big gorilla sleeping on the fallen tree.

He gently nudges the big gorilla. Wake up, sleepy head. It doesn't. It just stretches and turns over on its other side.

Thud!

The big gorilla falls off the tree and lands on its head.

That's got to hurt.

The big gorilla isn't a happy camper. It starts pounding its chest, making angry gorilla noises that sound like gorilla swears: SON-OF-A-OO-AH-AH!

Hambone sniffs.

"Oh, poor wittle gowilla," he says. "All mad because he bonked his wittle head. Boo-hoo."

But that's not how I would describe the way the big gorilla is acting. Mad is not a strong enough word—he's going ballistic.

Evil Doctor Crazy Gorilla nonchalantly walks over and stands face to face with the big gorilla.

"Is he out of his mind?" I say. "Or does he have a death wish?"

Neither, it turns out.

Evil Doctor Crazy Gorilla stands motionless in front of the big gorilla. Not moving a single muscle. Not even an eyelash as he stares into the big gorilla's eyes.

It's as if he is a gorilla whisperer.

Settle down big boy

Attempting to communicate calming thoughts without speaking. And it works. The big gorilla eventually calms down.

"That was amazing," I say. "Maybe I should start calling him Evil Doctor Crazy Gorilla whisperer."

"More like Evil Doctor Crazy Gorilla lover," says Hambone. "Loves gorillas that's all. I bet he's even the president of the Gorilla Fan Club of America."

"What do you think he's saying now?"

"Probably how much he loves him and how nobody understands how hard it is to be a gorilla...blah blah blah."

Whatever he said, it makes the big

gorilla lean its head back and open its mouth like a baby bird about to get its food from its mother.

"Got bananas?" I say.

Evil Doctor Crazy Gorilla reaches into the front pocket of his lab coat and takes out one of those old-fashioned medicine bottles. He removes the cork stopper. Greenish smoke billows out.

"See?" I say. "He's got some sort of potion there. I knew it. He really is a mad scientist."

"Whatever," says Hambone dismissively.

Geez, after all the times I've patted him on the back you'd think he could return the favor.

Anyway, Evil Doctor Crazy Gorilla carefully turns the old-fashioned medicine bottle upside down and pours some of the green potion into the big gorilla's mouth.

Wait for it. Wait for it.

Hmm.

Nothing happens.

That's a bummer.

Chapter Five

How Many Zombie Gorillas Does it Take to Change a Lightbulb?

What a difference a few seconds makes.

Something does happen.

Suddenly the big gorilla looks different.

The more I look at him, the more he doesn't look like any gorilla I know. It's like how my mom doesn't look like any mom I know when I forget to flush the toilet. She looks different. Like she wants to flush me down the toilet. And that's how the big gorilla looks now.

"This can't be good," I say.

And I'm right.

The big gorilla starts convulsing.

34

As if it's having a seizure. Then, just like that, its body stops convulsing and goes motionless. All stiff like.

"I think whatever Evil Doctor Crazy Gorilla gave that big gorilla just killed him," I say.

I wish.

The reason I wish is because of what happens next. After a few minutes of lying stiff as a board, the gorilla gets up. Its body suddenly changes, morphing from a gorilla into a...into a...no...this can't be happening. Its eyes turn bloodshot and bulge out of its head. Its jaw drops open, and its canine teeth grow into huge yellow fangs. Its chest sinks in, and its arms and legs shrivel up into deformed limbs. Its fur turns from black to gray and sags off his bones. Blood dribbles out of a gash opening up on its forehead. The gorilla isn't just some ordinary gorilla anymore. No. I can't believe I'm going to tell

35

you this. But now it's a...zombie gorilla!

"*Hambone, I've a feeling we're not in Tigertown anymore,*" I say.

"Relax," he says.

"Relax? I'll relax when we're miles away from this place."

"Are you kidding?" says Hambone. "I'm not leaving. I came here to unleash Dog Fu on that big gorilla who threw dirt at me, and that's what I'm going to do."

"Even if it's now a zombie?" I say.

"That's even better," says Hambone. "I hate zombies just as much as I hate gorillas."

It's true. He does.

"Well, be that as it may," I say. "Zombies and gorillas—those are two things I don't ever want to say in the same sentence. We should have been gone ten seconds ago."

Hambone stands up straight and crosses his arms over his chest. He's not going anywhere.

"Fine," I say. "Stay here if you want. I'm going."

But I don't move. I can't move. It's as if my legs are stuck in mud. Or worse—quicksand. And it feels like the more I try to move, the more I'm getting sucked down deeper into the quicksand.

Being in such close proximity to a zombie gorilla will do that to you, believe me.

"You still here?" says Hambone.

"My legs are stuck."

"Stuck?" Hambone smirks and then starts flapping his arms. "Bock. Bock."

"You're calling me a chicken?"

"Well, aren't you? I mean, look at you. You're so scared you can't even move."

"Oh, forgive me. What was I thinking? I should be jumping up and down shouting, 'Yeah! Zombie gorillas!' at the top of my lungs. So sorry. There must be something wrong with me."

"Well," says Hambone, "if you really want to know—"

"Wait," I say. "What is he doing now?"

Evil Doctor Crazy Gorilla goes over to each of the sleeping gorillas, gently nudging them awake and giving them some of the green potion.

Oh-My-Shneggies!

Now there's even more zombie gorillas.

They hoot and beat their chests and slap at the ground. Then they slowly swarm around Evil Doctor Crazy Gorilla, staggering as they knuckle walk.

I gulp. "How about now? Still staying? Math isn't my best subject, but I'd say thirty zombie gorillas is way more than one."

"Still not enough to change a lightbulb," says Hambone, smiling.

"Very funny," I say. "But what's not funny is how fast I get out of here."

Hambone gives me a look.

"What?"

"Your legs are stuck, remember?"

He's right.

But I have to get out of here somehow. There's no telling what Evil Doctor Crazy Gorilla and these zombie gorillas are up to.

Probably no good. And I'm right.

Evil Doctor Crazy Gorilla does more of his gorilla-whisperer stuff on the zombie gorillas. And then, as if everything that has happened up to this point weren't messed up enough, what happens next is even more messed up.

The zombie gorillas arrange themselves into rows. One in front of the other. Like an army amassing at the border of a country they are going to invade. Which makes Evil Doctor Crazy Gorilla the general in charge of the troops—waiting for the right moment to give the order to attack.

Like now.

I throw my hands up to the sky. "Darn this quicksand!" I cry.

"You know, Peas," says Hambone, shaking his head at me. "You're not really stuck in quicksand." He taps the side of his head. "It's all in your mind."

Try telling that to my legs.

I take a deep breath.

Must. Go. Now.

I grab my right leg with both hands and pull as hard as I can.

Ffsuuuuuuuup!

I free my right leg from the grip of the quicksand. I do the same with my left leg. Before I know it, I'm on solid ground and running as fast as I can. As far away from Evil Doctor Crazy Gorilla and those zombie gorillas as my little legs will take me.

CHAPTER SIX

I'll Get by With a Little Help From My Friends

"Helloooooo. Hellooooooooo in there. Come out, come out, wherever you are. Helloooooooooooooo!"

I don't answer Hambone. Why not? Because I know what's coming next. It's not Dog Fu he's going to unleash on me, but worse. He's going to unleash the ancient martial art known as busting-chops.

"Go away," I say. "Leave me alone."

"Aw," says Hambone, using his best baby voice. "What's the matter, little Peas? Did the big bad zombie gorillas make you want to go 'wee, wee, wee' all the way home?"

43

See what I mean? Busting chops. When it comes to busting chops, Hambone is the best. They should give him a medal. Call it the Royal Order of Chop Busting.

"That's not very cool," I say. "What if I was truly traumatized by what I saw? I could be scarred for life. You wouldn't be busting my chops then, would you?"

"Maybe," says Hambone.

"Really? Thanks a bunch."

"My pleasure."

"Not that I hope it makes you feel bad," I say. "But I wouldn't bust your chops if you were truly traumatized."

"You couldn't even if you wanted to."

"Why not?"

"Because I'd report you to the ASPCA quicker than you can say Jack Robinson. Busting my chops? That's cruelty to animals."

Hambone laughs.

I have to give him credit—he is the best.

But that doesn't mean I'm not annoyed by it.

"Go away!" I yell.

45

"Come on," says Hambone. "Stop being such a baby. I promise no more busting your chops. Just come on out of there, OK?"

I reluctantly crawl out from under my back porch.

"I'm surprised to see you here," I say.

"Why's that?" says Hambone.

"I thought you were having so much fun with those zombie gorillas," I say, still a little annoyed. "I thought you might want to stay with them and roast marshmallows over a nice, warm fire. Maybe sing 'Kumbaya' while you're at it."

"That sounds like fun."

"So why aren't you still there?"

"Because I missed you," he says, giving me a big hug. He lets go, but then squeezes me again. Tighter. Then he leans in and

46

whispers in my ear, *"You complete me."* 🎬

Even with a line from *Johnny Maloney* it's hard to tell if he's still busting my chops. But even still, the hug is nice. If you really want to know the truth, seeing those gorillas turn into zombie gorillas scared me.

"You complete me, too," I say. "But you start in on me again, and I go right back to where I was. I swear."

"Don't worry," says Hambone. "No more busting chops."

"Good," I say. "So what do we do now?"

"What do you mean?"

"Seriously?" I say, giving him a look. "Evil Doctor Crazy Gorilla is turning ordinary gorillas into zombie gorillas, and you're giving me 'What do you mean?' You saw the way those zombie gorillas were maneuvering—getting into tactical

47

formation. They're going to take over the world. One person at a time."

"Zombies shmombies," he says. "I'm so sick of hearing about zombies."

One of Hambone's rants is coming on. He does this. So get ready.

"Zombie this and zombie that," he continues. "Everywhere you look—there's a zombie. Zombie movies. Zombie TV shows. Zombie books. Zombie video games. I'm surprised there isn't a zombie cereal.

Just think of it: the cereal pieces could be shaped like severed heads. Yum, yum, yum. Braaaains! I'm surprised some marketing genius hasn't thought of it already."

Hambone stops. He's worked himself up so much he's exhausted. His tongue lolls out of his mouth.

I wait for him to cool down.

"What a day," continues Hambone. "All I wanted was to unleash some Dog Fu on that gorilla that threw dirt at me, and now this—zombie gorillas. Boy, could it get any worse?"

"Yes!" I say. "Yes, it can!"

Hambone ignores me. "I mean, did I do something to somebody in a previous life? Are they looking at me and laughing? Pointing and saying, 'Ha! Ha! You hate gorillas and zombies? Well, guess what?

We put the two together just for you—have fun!'?"

"What's so fun about zombie gorillas?"

Hambone continues to ignore me. "I guess I should look on the bright side. I have a chance to unleash some Dog Fu on the two things I hate most in the world. This might actually be a pretty good day after all. So what do you say?"

"Oh? So now you're talking to me?"

"Come, on," says Hambone, putting his paw on my shoulder. "Let's do this. Let's go unleash some Dog Fu on every single one of those zombie gorillas."

"I don't think that's a good idea," I say.

"Why not?" he says. "We have to do something. You said yourself that they looked like they were getting ready to attack. Maybe even trying to take over the

50

world. So let's unleash the Dog Fu, and that will be that. No more zombie gorillas."

"How much Dog Fu can you unleash?" I say, exasperated.

"What does that have to do with anything?" he says.

"We're not just dealing with one zombie gorilla here," I say. "There were what, maybe thirty or so of them? And that's just the beginning."

"The beginning?"

"Yeah, the beginning. That's the thing about zombies you don't know because you're too busy hating them. But I know a lot about them. I'm somewhat of an expert."

"Reads one book and suddenly he's an expert?" says Hambone out of the corner of his mouth.

"What was that?" I say.

"Nothing. I can't wait to hear everything you know about zombies."

"Well, first off, zombies need to feed on human flesh. So these zombie gorillas are going to start attacking people. And when they do, those people will also turn into zombie gorillas, and before you know it— zombie gorillas, zombie gorillas everywhere. And I don't know about you but I don't think unleashing Dog Fu is the answer. I think we should get some help."

"Help?" says Hambone, raising an eyebrow. "Who's going to help us?"

"Plenty of people," I say.

"People are useless," he says.

"Oh, yeah? What about the police?"

"Useless."

"How about the workers at the zoo?"

"Useless."

"Parents?"

"Useless."

"Teachers?"

"Beyond useless."

"Friends?"

Hambone shakes his head. "Contrary to public opinion, I do know a little something about zombies. But since you're the zombie expert, you tell me: What happens to most people when zombies attack?"

"I told you. They get turned into zombies. That's why—"

Hambone cuts me off. "So in other words, they're basically useless. Unless you want to go to a zombie for help, which I don't think you want to do."

"No. Of course not."

"So doesn't that mean it's just you and me, pal? The two of us? The two amigos? Saving the world from the attack of the zombie gorillas?"

"Yeah, I guess so." I hate to admit it, but he's right. I mean, every story has to have a hero. Somebody readers can root for. Somebody who saves the day. So I guess that's me and Hambone. We are the heroes of this story. But boy, what a depressing thought. Heroes sometimes die, you know.

"Hey, cheer up, buttercup," says Hambone, coming over to me and putting his arm around my shoulder. "This isn't going to be so bad. It'll be over before you know it. And then, guess what? We'll be famous. We'll be the guys who rid the world of zombie gorillas. Just think, people will give us money, Lamborghinis, diamonds, whatever we want."

"You know what I really want?" I say.

"What?"

"I want an ax. Not Dog Fu—that isn't going to cut it. If we're going to do this, if we're going to stop these zombie gorillas, we need something to smash their heads in to get to their brains. That's how you stop them for real."

"That's the spirit," says Hambone, lightly shaking my shoulders. "So what do you say we get us that ax."

"Where?"

Hambone points over my shoulder. "To your dad's shed."

CHAPTER SEVEN

IT'S A BIRD! IT'S A PLANE!
IT'S COUCH POTATO MAN!

My dad's this big gardener. Likes to spend his weekends gardening. So he bought this shed a couple of years ago to keep all his tools in. The shed is enormous. It looks like a miniature house right in our backyard.

"I don't know why you guys put me in that puny doghouse," says Hambone, stopping in front of the shed. "I should be living here. Boy, I bet a family of oompa loompas could live in here comfortably."

I go to open the shed door. But there's a combination lock on it.

"When did your dad put that on?" says Hambone.

"I don't know," I say. "And I also don't know the combination. This isn't good. My dad doesn't get home from work until five o'clock. That's like twenty hours from now in zombie gorilla time."

"Don't worry. I can pick that thing in like thirty seconds flat."

"You know how to pick a lock? I didn't know you knew how to do that."

"I know all sorts of things."

58

"I can't pick anything."

"Don't sell yourself short. You're an expert at picking your nose."

"Hey, that's not fair. I can't help it if I have bad sinuses. It's genetic. Blame my parents."

Hambone sniffs. Then he goes over to our recycle bin on the back porch. He rummages through it and comes out with a soda can. He bites into the can, tearing off a jagged piece of aluminum. He folds the jagged piece over into the shape of a triangle. Then he folds it again into a smaller triangle.

"That should do it," says Hambone.

"What should do what?" I say.

"Just watch." He goes over to the combination lock. He sticks the aluminum triangle piece he made into the curved metal bar. He takes it out. Then he sticks it back in again, only harder. Kind of like he's trying to jam it into the curved metal bar. He keeps jamming it until—boing! The lock opens.

"That was amazing," I say.

"Save your applause," says Hambone, walking into the shed.

"I think what we're looking for is hanging up on the walls," I say, following right behind him.

"Holy smokes," he says. "Are you kidding me with this place?"

Nobody's kidding anybody. Except maybe my dad. The reason I say this is because we don't find any gardening tools. Instead we find a flat-screen TV, a mini-fridge stocked with beer, a lounge chair with compartments filled with potato chips and beef jerky—all hooked up to a generator.

"This isn't a shed," says Hambone. "This is a man cave."

"No wonder he spends all his time in here," I say.

"I have to hand it to your dad," he says. "I didn't think he had it in him. But what a perfect scam. He had me fooled."

"Me, too," I say. "Wow, I can't believe he's scamming us."

"Maybe he's not scamming at all," he says. "Maybe he's a superhero—Couch Potato Man. And he has the power to sit on his butt all day and not spend time with his family. Instead of up, up, and away, it's sit, sit, and veg."

"That doesn't make me feel better," I say.

In one corner of the shed, we actually do find an ax and a pick shovel. So maybe I can give my dad some credit for at least keeping up appearances.

"Which one do you want?" says Hambone.

I take the ax and give Hambone the pick shovel. Then we lock the shed back up on our way out.

The ax feels kind of heavy in my hand. I'm not really sure I'll be able to wield it when the time comes.

I practice swinging it a couple times.

It drops out of my hand.

Not because I lost my grip but because my grip lost me. What I mean is, this sudden shock zaps my body, a bolt of electricity causing all my muscles to suddenly stop working.

Hambone notices this.

"What's the matter?" he says.

I try to speak, but I can't. The shock has worn off, but for some reason it has left the muscles in my face useless. All I can do is try to act out what I want to say. Like charades.

"OK," says Hambone, picking up on what's happening. "How many words?"

I put up two fingers.

"First word?" he says.

I stick my arms straight out.

"You're tired."

I shake my head. I start groaning.

"You're tired, and you feel sick to your stomach."

I shake my head. I put up two fingers again.

"OK," he says. "Second word."

I hop on one leg and then the other, doing this little jig-like dance.

"You have a hot foot?" he says. "No. You'd be jumping up and down on only one foot. Two hot feet? No. You're stepping on hot coals? How about ants in your pants?"

Seriously? I shake my head. Then I try to think of another clue. I start pounding my chest as I do my jig-like dance.

64

"You have heartburn?" He keeps guessing. "Indigestion? Wait—I got it? You're choking on a piece of food? No? What?"

Maybe it's because of Hambone's astounding stupidity. Or maybe it's because my face muscles are no longer useless. But I can speak again.

"Look behind you!" I scream.

Hambone turns around.

Standing right in front of him is a squad of zombie gorillas.

CHAPTER EIGHT

EVERYBODY WAS
DOG FU FIGHTING

I try to remember the last time I saw Hambone falling from that high in the air.

I think it was when he fell out of the tree in Mrs. Madigan's yard.

He was chasing Mrs. Madigan's cat. That cat was pretty smart. She went all the way to the top of the tree figuring Hambone wouldn't have the guts to follow. But he did. And as he was just about to sink his teeth into little Fluffylufugus, he slipped and fell, plummeting to the ground. When he hit, he sat up all dazed like. And I swear I could see little birdies circling around his head. Just like in the cartoons.

I wonder if I'll see them again when he lands this time.

Wait a second. I shouldn't be thinking that.

I should be horrified that just a moment ago one of the zombie gorillas grabbed Hambone and flung him about thirty feet into the air.

He's on his way down now.

Three. Two. One.

THUD!

Hambone sits up.

Nope. No little birdies this time.

But he's definitely dazed.

"Holly mother of..." says Hambone. But he doesn't have the chance to finish his sentence. That's because another zombie gorilla knocks him to the ground and starts stomping on his back.

"I...could...use...a...little...help...here," gasps Hambone in between stomps.

I reach down for my ax. It feels like it weighs a ton. With every muscle in my body straining, I lift the ax over my head and— SMASH! Right down on the zombie gorilla's oversized noggin.

Its skull cracks open like a watermelon dropped from a tall building onto the sidewalk below. But instead of yummy, pulpy-pink stuff splattering everywhere, it's just the opposite. This oozy mixture of brain and snot and pus splatters all over me. It's on my clothes. In my hair. Little bitty chunks even stick to my face.

I wipe off what I can, but it's not good enough.

The smell.

Makes you lose your appetite smelling that smell, believe me. You might even lose something else—like your lunch.

I try not to breathe.

But I have to. Obviously.

"Don't just stand there," says Hambone, shaking off the pain. "There's more where that one came from."

He's right.

"Watch out," I say.

Another zombie gorilla lurches at Hambone. But he thinks fast. He squats down and whips his leg out, chopping the legs out from under the zombie gorilla.

"Wow!" I say. "Was that Dog Fu?"

"Maybe," says Hambone.

"Come on. You can tell me. It's not a secret is it?"

"First rule of Dog Fu is: You do not talk about Dog Fu." 🎬

Well, maybe Hambone will have something to say about that zombie gorilla that's knuckle walking up to him. "You're going to need this," I say, tossing the ax over to him. "And remember, you have to get to his brain."

Hambone does just that.

More of that oozy mixture splatters out.

"You're going to want to hold your nose," I say. "That stuff reeks."

Hambone tosses the ax back to me. "You're going to want to hold that," he says, nodding toward something behind me. "Zombie gorilla—ten o'clock."

I turn and swing my ax at the same time, hoping to make contact with the zombie gorilla.

But I only make contact with air. What the…?

I look down.

Oh, so that's why. It's a baby zombie gorilla.

Awww. How cute.

But it isn't cute what that baby zombie gorilla does next.

It smiles and then grabs my…it…um… well…how do I put this politely? I could…but. Um…OK…I guess I'll just come out and say it: it grabs my private parts.

"Hey, that's not fair grabbing a kid down there," I say, my voice suddenly high-pitched and squeaky.

"All's fair in love and war with flesh-eating zombie gorillas," says Hambone, rushing up to help me.

He gives the baby zombie gorilla a forearm shiver to the neck, sending it tumbling backward.

"See what you get? See what you get when you mess with the Dog Fu?"

Obviously in all the excitement, Hambone forgot what I told him—unleashing Dog Fu isn't going to have any effect on a zombie gorilla. Even a baby zombie gorilla.

Speaking of which, that baby zombie gorilla Hambone knocked backward is now up on its feet, dusting itself off. It turns sideways, spreads its legs farther apart, and bends its knees. Girding itself for a fight.

"Don't look now," I say.

The baby zombie gorilla waves
Hambone to come at it.

"Is it challenging me?" he says.

"I think so," I say.

"It's challenging me," he says again.
"Unbelievable."

"Remember," I say. "Pick shovel—not
Dog Fu."

Luckily, the pick shovel is within Hambone's reach. He bends down and picks it up.

"Here little baby zombie gorilla," he says. "Come to Hambone and get your brains smashed in."

He swings the pick shovel around his body, passing it from paw to paw as it goes around and around. Like that Bruce Lee kung-fu guy with the nunchucks. Then Hambone passes the pick shovel over and under each arm. Again and again. Getting faster each time he does it.

(He's doing some serious kung-fu stuff now. Bruce Lee has nothing on Hambone.)

The baby zombie gorilla doesn't know what to do. It's torn. Should it wait for Hambone to come at it, or is it going to have to go at Hambone? It decides to go at

Hambone. But I don't think it really wants to. It gingerly steps closer to Hambone. Like a kid on the beach testing the ocean with his toes to see how cold the water is. It steps even closer but then jumps back when the pick shovel almost whacks it.

"What's a matter, baby zombie gorilla?" says Hambone. "You scared? Are you a scared baby zombie gorilla?"

The baby zombie gorilla grunts.

Hambone sniffs. "Come on," he says. "Come closer again. I dare you."

More grunting.

"What if I do this?" says Hambone, resting the pick shovel on his shoulder.

"I wouldn't do that if I were you," I warn.

Seeing this as his chance to get at Hambone, the baby zombie gorilla opens its mouth wide and lunges forward.

"WATCHAAAW," yells Hambone as he whacks the baby zombie gorilla right between the eyes.

It crumples to the ground with the pick shovel still stuck in its head.

"Holy Moly," I say. "That was amazing."

"I'll give you an autograph later," says Hambone. "But for now let's get smashing."

CHAPTER NINE

THESE BRAINS ARE MAKING ME THIRSTY!

Turns out Hambone is a lot better at smashing zombie gorillas than I am.

I'm still having trouble lifting the ax over my head.

Maybe if I do some of that kung-fu stuff Hambone was doing earlier.

Ouch!

Maybe not.

Every time I try to pass the ax around my body it ends up hitting me in the butt.

Hurts like a...but that's not the worst part. The worst part of it is the zombie gorillas think I'm a fool.

(It's bad enough that every kid at my

school thinks I'm a fool, but now zombie gorillas as well?!?)

"What are you doing over there, Peas?" says Hambone.

"I'm doing my best, but they're laughing at me," I say. "See? They have these big smiles on their faces."

"I think that means they like you," he says.

(Now is definitely not the time for busting chops.)

That's because a zombie gorilla is coming right at me.

Here goes nothing.

"WOOOOOOOO-ooooOOOO-WAHHHHHHHH!" I yell. Why not?

Luckily, it works. I swing the ax and smash the zombie gorilla in the head. And then I smash another and another.

"How many are there?" I say.

"I don't know," says Hambone. "Why don't you ask them? Maybe invite them to stay for tea while you're at it."

"I'm just saying."

"Well, stop saying and start smashing."

I do.

But it's weird. I could swear one of the zombie gorillas I smashed is the same one I smashed earlier. The same one whose brain chunks are still on my clothes.

Could it really be the same zombie gorilla? Is that even possible?

I have to know. It's killing me. I need scientifically verifiable proof. (*When I grow up, I'm going to be a scientist—I have a keen scientific mind.*)

I decide to conduct an experiment. I taste one of the chunks on my clothes and then compare the taste with a chunk of brain from the zombie gorilla I just smashed.

Yup. They taste the same.

You know what this means, don't you? These zombie gorillas are somehow coming back to life even after getting their brains smashed in.

OH-MY-SHNEGGIES!

They're regenerating!

If that's the case, how do you stop them? The answer is there is no stopping them.

Speaking of which, another squadron of zombie gorillas invades our backyard. A blitzkrieg of gray fur and yellow fangs seemingly coming from all directions. Over the grass. From out under the porch. Some swinging down from tree branches. Some even jumping off the roof of my dad's shed. All headed in our direction. If me and Hambone don't get out of here, the next sentence you're going to read will be one describing the excruciating pain caused by a zombie gorilla biting off your flesh.

"Retreat! Retreat!" I yell.

"Retreat?" says Hambone. "Never."

"We don't stand a chance."

"Speak for yourself."

"What do you mean?"

Hambone holds the pick shovel up over his head.

He can't be serious.

"You're going to need a bigger pick shovel." 🎬

Hambone looks at the squadron of zombie gorillas getting closer. "You're right," he says. "Let's get out of here."

Chapter Ten

Leggo My Eggo...Elves

As we're running away across Baskin Field, I hear this sound overhead.

I don't believe my eyes. It's a World War I fighter plane. The only World War I fighter plane I know of belongs to Mr. Oswalt. He's this crazy old guy in our neighborhood who thinks he's a flying ace in World War I. Kind of like Snoopy thinking he's battling his archenemy, the Red Baron. But Mr. Oswalt isn't sitting on top of his doghouse claiming he's flying a Sopwith Camel—he went out and bought a real one.

And that's the plane now heading directly toward us.

Oh-my-shneggies!

The upper and lower wings look like giant knife blades. The propeller, the blade in a blender. That's a lot of blades.

Which isn't good. Not if you want to stay in one piece.

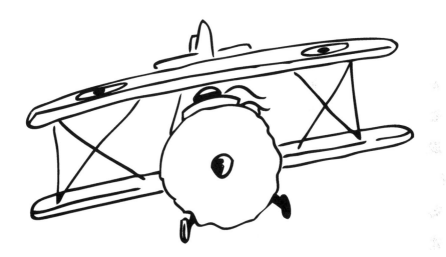

We dive to the ground and cover our heads with our hands—just in time.

WHOOSH!

The plane flies over, trailing a wave of air that nearly lifts us off the ground.

"What's he doing?" says Hambone. "Is

he trying to kill us?"

The plane circles around and comes back in our direction.

"I don't know," I say. "But let's not wait around and find out."

We get up and start running—as fast as our little legs will take us.

Ouch!

I turn my ankle in a sinkhole and fall, smacking my face right into the ground.

That's going to leave a big mark.

"Get up," says Hambone, turning to look at me but not stopping.

I can't get up. To be honest with you, I'm a little dazed. Like cartoon-seeing-birdies dazed. Yup. There they are now.

"Come back, pretty birdies," I say.

Hambone turns and sees me still on the ground, so he stops.

"Here, pretty birdies," I say.

"What are you talking about?" says Hambone, rushing to my aid. He picks me up, puts me on his shoulder, and starts running again.

"Don't you see the pretty birdies?" I say.

"I don't see any birdies," he says. "All I see is a plane heading straight for us."

He runs faster.

WHOOSH!

The plane passes just inches above our heads.

The wave of air this time causes Hambone to stumble and fall. When he lands on the ground, he lets go of me, and I tumble forward a few yards more.

Which isn't the most wonderful experience considering I'm still feeling a little dazed.

"Look at the pretty birdies," I say.

"Enough with the birdies," says Hambone.

"But they're so pretty."

"Enough!"

I snap out of it.

Just in time to watch the plane as it

lands on the soccer field, does a pirouette, and taxis right up to us.

Mr. Oswalt turns off the engine and climbs out of the cockpit.

He's dressed in full flying-ace regalia:

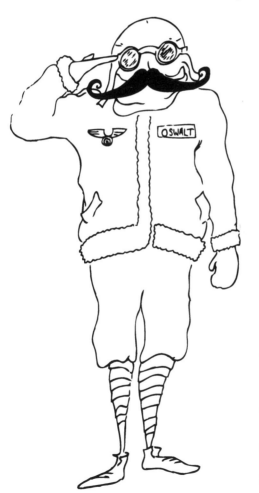

leather bomber jacket, aviator helmet, goggles, and a red scarf.

"I heard a great deal of commotion in the neighborhood," says Mr. Oswalt. "Are the Germans on the attack again?"

"Germans?" I say. "They aren't Germans, Mr. Oswalt. They're zombie gorillas."

"Now, now, young man," says Mr. Oswalt. "I know there's a tendency in the heat of battle to disparage the enemy. But it's not becoming a gentleman to resort to name calling. Actually, it's downright uncivilized."

"Boy, this old guy really is off his rocker," whispers Hambone.

I elbow him in the ribs.

"I'm just saying," whispers Hambone. "Besides, you don't need to elbow me. Even if I were to jump up and down reciting the Gettysburg Address in front of ole Mr. Out-of-His-Mind here, he'd still wouldn't suspect a thing. Our secret is safe with us."

He's right. But still. We don't want to

push it.

"Where is the enemy now?" says Mr. Oswalt.

"Back there somewhere," I say, pointing over my shoulder. "But I hope we've lost them. The last thing I want to see right now is a zombie gorilla."

"Language, young man," says Mr. Oswalt. "Remember your language."

"But you don't understand," I say. "These zombie gorillas…er…um…I mean, the Germans—if they catch up to us—are going to eat our flesh off."

"I got an idea," says Hambone, pulling me off to the side so Mr. Oswalt won't hear. "Ask him to go back up in his plane and go after those zombie gorillas for us."

"What's that going to do?" I say. "You have to smash their brains in, remember?"

"You see an ax or pick shovel around here?" says Hambone.

Uh-oh. We dropped them back at our house when we retreated.

"That plane is the best weapon we have right now," continues Hambone. "At the very least, he'll keep them occupied so we can find new ones."

"OK," I say. "I'll give it a try."

(If there's one thing I know how to do, it's talk to crazy old people. I've had a lot of practice with my grandfather. He's even crazier than Mr. Oswalt. How much crazier? My grandfather thinks he's the King of Waffle Land and I'm his loyal subject, Bob.)

"Wow, that sure is a neat plane you have there, Mr. Oswalt," I say. "I bet you could shoot down a lot of Germans with that plane."

Mr. Oswalt stands taller.

"I have forty-nine confirmed kills," he says, beaming. "Of course, when you are as skilled as I am, your fellow aces get jealous. Did you know they tried to steal my Distinguished Flying Crosses? How dare they? Each one was awarded personally to me by His Majesty King George V."

Now it's Hambone's turn to elbow me in the ribs. He points insistently to the plane.

"I know," I say. "But it takes time. You can't just come out and ask. You don't know how they might react."

(One time my grandfather threw waffles at my head because he was mad at me for forgetting that Waffle Land was once ruled by the evil Eggo Elves.)

"What was that, young man?" says Mr. Oswalt. "Are you saying something?

Speak up."

"Right," I say. "Sorry. Um...have you ever heard of a place called Waffle Land?"

"I have never heard of such a place, young man," says Mr. Oswalt. "Is it under enemy attack?"

"No," I say. "But who knows what the evil Eggo Elves are up to!"

Hambone howls.

"What?" I say.

"Seriously?" he whispers. "Well, you can stay here chitchatting with Commander Cuckoo Bird if you want, but I'm not going to let a

perfectly good plane go to waste. See you."

"Get back here," I say, out of the corner of my mouth.

Hambone doesn't listen. Instead, he sneaks around Mr. Oswalt unnoticed and heads for the plane. When he gets there he smiles, waves good-bye, and jumps into the cockpit.

"Um, excuse me, Mr. Oswalt," I say. "I'll be right back. Why don't you stand guard and let us know if you see any Germans approaching."

"Excellent idea," says Mr. Oswalt, snapping to attention and saluting me.

I rush over to Hambone.

"What are you doing?" I say.

"What does it look like I'm doing?" he says. "You want something done you have

95

to do it yourself."

"Come, on. Get out of there. What if Mr. Oswalt catches you?"

"Are you kidding? Just look at him."

It's hard to put into words what exactly Mr. Oswalt is doing. But if I had to, I'd say it's a cross between marching and catching butterflies with an imaginary net.

"Fine," I say. "But it's not like you know how to fly this thing."

"I don't?" says Hambone, giving me a look.

"Seriously?" I say. "Where'd you learn–Snoopy's Flying Ace Academy?"

"Wouldn't you like to know," says Hambone. "But that's not important right now."

He's right.

What's important is that the zombie gorillas have found us again.

CHAPTER ELEVEN

HANG IN THERE, PEAS!

I can't believe my eyes.

"Look, Mr. Oswalt," I say, pointing at the other end of the field. "The Germans are coming. Shouldn't you get in your plane and stop them?"

Mr. Oswalt keeps marching and catching imaginary butterflies.

Boy, he really is out of it.

Now what?

Hambone turns on the engine and grabs the yoke. "I'll show those zombie gorillas a thing or two," he says. *"They may eat our brains but they'll never take our freedom."* 🎬

"Come on, Hambone," I say. "Enough fooling around. Get out of there."

Suddenly, Mr. Oswalt knocks me to the ground. "Battle stations!" he yells. "Battle stations!"

"Wait, Mr. Oswalt," I say.

He doesn't. He reaches into the cockpit, takes Hambone by the collar, and tosses him to the ground.

"Look at the pretty little lady doggies," says Hambone, obviously dazed.

I laugh. Pretty little lady doggies? That's funny.

Hambone shakes it off. "What happened?"

"You got Dog Fu'd."

Mr. Oswalt jumps into the cockpit. He throws his red scarf over his shoulder and places his goggles over his eyes. He gives us the thumbs-up sign. Then he revs the engine.

I cover my ears.

Mr. Oswalt starts singing above the roar of the engine. "Off we go into the wild blue yonder, up, up, and away!"

I stand and salute Mr. Oswalt. Don't ask me why. It just feels like the right thing to do.

The plane moves forward.

I look back at the zombie gorillas. They're almost right upon us. A few more seconds, and we'll be...No. I won't even entertain the thought. It's too gruesome.

The plane picks up speed.

I look at Hambone.

He looks at me.

We both look at the plane.

"Are you thinking what I'm thinking?" I say.

He is. We run over to the plane, trying to catch up to it before it takes off into the air.

We make it.

I grab hold of one of the wires bracing the upper and lower wings. I pull myself up onto the lower wing. Hambone does the same thing on the other side.

Phew! That was close. Now all we have to do is sit and wait until we land—holding on tight to the wires, of course.

Off we go. Up, up, and away. Just like the words Mr. Oswalt is singing.

I sing along with him. So does Hambone.

All of a sudden, the plane tilts violently to one side.

I'm sliding down the wing, my arms stretching to their popping point as I desperately hold onto the wire.

The plane tilts violently to the other side.

Now I'm scrunched up against the wire, my cheek pressed into it. That's going to leave a bigger mark.

"Don't look now," says Hambone.

I look.

Oh-my-shneggies!

I don't believe my eyes. Two zombie gorillas are sitting on either side of the plane's tail, rocking it up and down. Like it's a teeter-totter.

How the...?

It doesn't matter. They're there—that's what matters.

And now the zombie gorilla on my side is up on its feet, getting ready to jump.

Where?

Onto the upper wing above me, it turns out. You've got to be kidding me!

The zombie gorilla swings back and forth as if it's in the jungle swinging on a tree branch.

WHAP!

It kicks me right in the kisser.

That's going to leave an even bigger mark.

WHAM!

Another kick to the face.

"Look, the little birdies are back," I say.

Come on, Peas. Snap out of it. You have to be strong.

But I'm not strong—I'm dazed.

I weeble backward.

I wobble forward.

I'm going to fall off the wing.

Before I do, I reach out, grasping for anything that might be in my reach.

Which turns out to be the zombie gorilla's dangling hand.

Gotcha!

Eww. This is one hairy zombie gorilla.

But other than that, it's not so bad. Hanging on to the zombie gorilla's hand like this kind of reminds me of traveling on a zip line. Zipping through the air. Wind on my face. What fun. I can do this all day if I have to.

Uh-oh.

I spoke too soon.

I'm slipping. Darn hairy hand.

No. It's not me. Then what is it?

Shoot.

It's the zombie gorilla. It can't hold on to the upper wing any longer. It's losing its grip.

Gradually...gradually...gone.

And down we go.

Down. Down. Down.

I close my eyes.

This is definitely going to leave the biggest mark yet.

Chapter Twelve

Don't Drink The Dum-Dum Juice

As it turns out, I'm one lucky son of a gun.

I'm not going to go splat on the ground. No broken bones. Mangled limbs. Skull fractures. Not going to spend months in a hospital bed laid up in traction, spoon-fed by some nurse with a mustache and breath that smells like sardines.

No. I'm going to be just fine.

How is that possible?

For one, we were actually flying awfully low to the ground. You can't fly

up, up and away when you have the added weight of two zombie gorillas to deal with. In fact, we were probably lucky we didn't crash.

For another, when I began my free fall, I just happened to be directly over the playground at my school.

I'm heading for the giant slide.

Talk about serendipity.

What better way to break my fall?

I reach out my arms Superman style. Look. It's a bird. It's a plane. It's me. Able to go down giant slides in a single glide.

Here we go.

I land smoothly on my stomach at the top of the slide.

Whee!

When I get to the bottom, my momentum shoots me back up into the air, where I do a back somersault with a twist and land perfectly on my feet.

Totally not on purpose.

Where's somebody with a cell when you need one? Put it up on WeTube. I'd go viral. Probably get way more views than Surprised Kitty.

Oh, well.

"Everything OK there?" says Hambone, calling over to me.

"Yeah, I'm fine," I say. "What happened to you?"

"When I saw you fall, I jumped for it," says Hambone. "Did you know the sand the kindergartners have in their sandbox is surprisingly soft?"

"I did not know that," I say.

"It is," says Hambone. "It's like fluffy pillow soft."

"Good to know," I say. "The next time I'm helplessly falling from a World War I fighter plane, I'll try to land in the sandbox."

"I recommend it."

"I recommend never having a next time," I say, dusting some sand out of Hambone's fur. "Just think, it could have been a whole lot worse."

"Tell that to him."

Hambone points to the zombie gorilla head swinging on the tetherball pole.

Aagh! Gross! I cover my nose.

"What are you doing?" says Hambone.

"What does it look like I'm doing? Can't you smell that?"

Hambone takes

a deep breath. *"Ahh. Love the smell of smashed-in zombie gorilla brains in the morning. Smells like—victory!"* 🎬

"I'm not so sure of that," I say, starting to walk away. "Come on, we better get out of here before he comes back to life."

Hambone gives me a look.

"What are you talking about?"

"Well," I say. "They don't stay dead, you know."

"Come again?"

"These zombie gorillas, there is something about them."

"Like what?"

"Well, normally you'd think you smash a zombie's brain in, that's it—it's all over. But not these guys. I'm telling you, back at the house I killed the same zombie gorilla

///

twice."

"How do you know it was the same zombie gorilla? It's hard to tell the difference between them."

"I know. That's why I needed to make sure. So I conducted a taste test—and both brains tasted the same to me."

Hambone gives me a look. "You ate zombie gorilla brains?"

"I needed proof," I say.

"That doesn't prove anything. Except that you've been drinking the dum-dum juice again. I mean, seriously, don't you think that all zombie gorilla brains taste the same? Why would one taste different from another?" He shakes his head. "You know, if you're still hungry, I have some yellow snow you can eat. Think of it as dessert. A lemon icy."

"Make fun if you want," I say, "but I still say these zombie gorillas can come back to life. Which means I don't know how we are going to stop them.  Which means we'll soon be living in a world run by zombie gorillas. I just wish I knew how it was possible for them to regenerate."

"Well, when you figure that out, please let me know," says Hambone, rolling his eyes. "But in the meantime, we have serious issues to deal with. In case you forgot, we still don't have any weapons."

I shake my head.

"What?" says Hambone. "You got something to say—spit it out."

"What good are weapons going to do if they just come back to life?"

"Again with that?"

"I'm just saying."

"Well what do you want to do—give up? Let those zombie gorillas eat us alive?"

"No, no. We have to do something."

"That's right. And the sooner the better. We have no idea where the other zombie gorillas are. They could be anywhere. They could be coming for us right now, for all we know."

"That's true," I say, nodding my head.

"I know it is," says Hambone. "And listen, don't take this the wrong way. I know you have a keen scientific mind and everything, but what if you're wrong about those zombie gorillas? Then what? Without weapons to smash their brains in, we're goners."

"No, I hear what you're saying," I say. "And I could be wrong. I don't think I am. But even if I'm right, smashing their brains in is the only thing we have going for us right now. I mean, what are we going to do if that one on the metal tetherball pole over there suddenly comes back to life, right?"

"Right," says Hambone, rubbing his paws together. "So let's go find us some weapons."

CHAPTER THIRTEEN

AND THE OSCAR GOES TO....HAMBONE!

Hambone walks over to the front entrance to the school.

"Where are you going?" I say. "It's summer—the school is closed."

"You forget about Skills and Thrills?" he says.

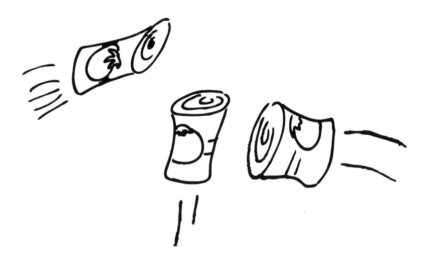

Skills and Thrills is a summer program for the kids who get into a lot of trouble at school. You know, the ones who make fart sounds in class or stick pencils up their noses or throw a can of tomato soup at the teacher.

(Swear. True story. Kenny Martin. Second grade. Stole the can of soup from the kitchen at school. Just missed Mr. Landell's head. Bounced off the blackboard and landed at my feet.)

The ones who basically spend their day in the principal's office. And so if you're not in class when you should be in class, they make you go to school over the summer and call it Skills and Thrills.

(I get the skills part, but I'm not so sure about the thrills. What's so thrilling about summer school? Do they get to throw cans of tomato soup at one another.)

I pause at the entrance. "We should have a plan, Hambone. In case we get caught."

Hambone pats me on the shoulder. "Life on the edge, Peas. Life on the edge."

We walk in the front entrance past the office.

"Hey! You're not allowed in here."

Uh-oh. That's Mrs. Wetbottom, the school's secretary.

"Quick! Play dead!" I say, pushing Hambone to the ground.

He looks up at me. "What was that for?"

"Do you want Mrs. Wetbottom to call the cops?" I say. "Or do you want to try and put one over on her?"

Hambone smirks. "Your deviousness

impresses me."

"Well, we don't really have a choice. Do we? We need weapons."

Hambone nods his head and winks. Then being the pro he is lets out this very dramatic howl and rolls onto his back. Sticking his legs straight up in the air as stiff as four pieces of wood.

I want to clap my hands and yell "Bravo! Bravo!" But I don't. Not with Mrs. Wetbottom walking right up to us.

"Young man, not only are you not allowed in school but there is absolutely, positively no dogs allowed, either."

"But can't you see he's sick," I say. "I think it's something he ate. Bad shrimp maybe."

She's not buying it. I need to think of something else. Something that would make Hambone proud.

"Please don't let anything happen to him," I say, giving her my saddest sad face. "He's my best friend in the whole world."

Mrs. Wetbottom just stares at me.

OK. OK. Looks like I better put on a show.

I drop to my knees and wrap my arms around Hambone's neck. "He's too young to die! Too young, I say! No. Never again will he rip apart our neighbor's garbage bag to

eat the dirty diapers.
Never again will he
chase his tail around
in circles until he
becomes so dizzy he
falls flat on his face.
Never again will he
chew up a bunch of
pine cones, put them

in a pile, then roll on top of them to scratch
his back. Boo-hoo. He'll never do anything
ever again. Oh, the horror. The inhumanity."

"Is she buying it?" Hambone whispers.

I peek up at Mrs.
Wetbottom.

You're not going
to believe this but
there are actually
tears in her eyes.
Slowly welling up

and rolling down her cheeks.

"Oh, no," she sobs. "I will not let anything happen to your dog, young man. I could not live with myself if I did. Let me go call the nurse. Maybe she can help."

Mrs. Wetbottom goes back into the office.

"Time to amscray," I say, pulling Hambone up by the collar.

We take off and head down the front hallway, going past the library and the cafeteria.

"This way," says Hambone, turning down another hallway.

"Where are we going?" I say.

"Custodian's office," he says. "That's our best bet."

I follow Hambone to the custodian's

office.

He knocks on the door. No answer. He knocks again. Still no answer.

"Coast is clear," says Hambone.

He opens the door and we go in.

"Wow," I say. "He sure does have a lot of stuff in here." And when I say stuff, I mean man-cave stuff. There's an aquarium with German blue rams and black skirt tetras. A dartboard. Weights. A remote-controlled monster truck. An indoor putting green. A neon lamp.

Wow. This place has everything.

There's even a pinup calendar hanging on the wall.

"Check this out," says Hambone, taking down the calendar and flipping through the months. "It's all custodians."

He shows me July. It's a picture of a custodian hugging a mop. His lips are puckered up. As if he's going to kiss the mop head. August has a custodian wrapping himself up in duck tape. October has a custodian wearing a ballerina costume.

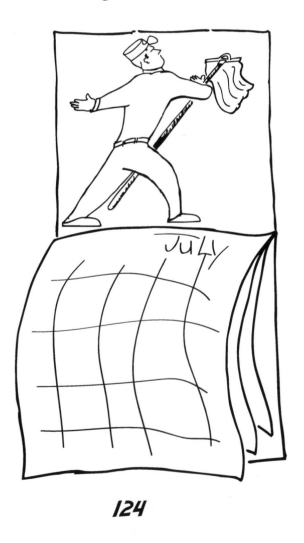

"Don't show me any more," I say.

"You have to see this one," says Hambone. It's December. There's a custodian dressed in a Santa suit on all fours scrubbing a toilet.

"My eyes," I say. "I'm blotting it out from my memory."

Hambone howls.

"Now I know what to get you for your birthday."

He puts the pinup calendar back on the wall and goes over to the tool chest in the corner.

"There better be something good in here."

There isn't.

All he finds are a hammer and a mallet.

"I guess it's better than nothing," says

Hambone, handing me the hammer and keeping the mallet for himself.

 The hammer feels like a toothpick in my hands. Oh, great. If a zombie gorilla has a piece of food stuck in his teeth, I'm all set.

I'm about to ask Hambone if he would like to switch weapons with me when I hear a voice behind us.

"What's going on in here?"

CHAPTER FOURTEEN

WHAT TO DO IN CASE OF A ZOMBIE ATTACK

I turn around.

Standing in the doorway with his hands on his hips is Mr. O'Dongle. Our custodian. Are you kidding me? Could it be any harder to sneak into school and get weapons?

"You have about three seconds to tell me what you think you're doing in my office," says Mr. O'Dongle. "And it better be the truth."

I look over at Hambone. He nods his approval.

"We need weapons," I say.

"Weapons?" says Mr. O'Dongle. "What do you need weapons for?"

I look over at Hambone again. He nods again.

Boy, how am I going to put this? If saying that Hambone is a dog that can walk and talk just like a kid will get me sent to the loony bin, then where will I get sent if I tell Mr. O'Dongle that there are flesh-eating zombie gorillas trying to take over the world?

Here goes nothing.

"Well, you see, we need weapons to kill the… um… well, you're not going to believe this but there are these gorillas… well, they're not really gorillas technically they are kind of sort of like… well, they're kind of like… um, like zombies."

"Zombies? Did you say zombies?" says Mr. O'Dongle, clasping his hands together and jumping up and down as if he's on a pogo stick. "Oh, goody, goody!"

I give Hambone a look. He shrugs his shoulders. Yeah, I agree, definitely not the reaction I was expecting. Can you say totally wacko?

Mr. O'Dongle starts pacing back and forth. "OK. Calm down. Get your body under control. Deep breath. In. Out. Good. Now, what's the first thing we need to do? The first thing we need to do is get our supplies ready."

"Supplies?" I say. "Supplies for what?"

"Why, to survive the zombie attack, of course." Mr. O'Dongle goes over to a locked cabinet attached to the wall. "Thank goodness I'm prepared. Warm blankets, water, freeze-dried food, first-aid kit, a solar charger, radar backpack, satellite radio. They are all in here." He opens the cabinet. "See?"

"I've been preparing for this day my entire life," he continues. "Those zombies aren't going to get me. No way. No how. I bet they're going to get that sales clerk. I bet he regrets giving me a funny look. I bet he wishes he has what I have. Too bad. Survival of the fittest." He grabs bottles of water. "How many of these do you think you can carry?"

"Um, I don't know," I say.

"Better pack as many as we can," he says, grabbing a giant duffle bag from the top shelf. He starts shoving in water bottles and other supplies.

"Boy," says Mr. O'Dongle. "This really is my lucky day. I can't believe how happy I am right now." He smiles and then starts singing, "I've got zombies on a zombie day. I bet you say what can make me feel this way? Zombies. Zombies. Talking about zombies."

As Mr. O'Dongle continues to sing and pack, I tiptoe over to Hambone.

"Does he expect us to go with him?"

"I don't know," whispers Hambone. "But I do know that we don't have time for this. We have to get out of here."

Hambone is right. Luckily, Mr. O'Dongle isn't paying any attention to us. He's too busy singing and packing.

"Let's sneak out of here," I say.

"Wait a second," says Hambone, grabbing a can of spray paint on his way out of the custodian's office. "We're going to need this, too."

"What's that for?"

"I've been thinking. We kind of need to know if you're right about that whole zombie-gorilla-coming-back-to-life thing. If you're right, we're in trouble. So I figure after we smash their brains in, we can spray a mark or something on their fur. Like a tag. And if we see any of those with that tag again, we'll know."

"So you believe me," I say, putting my hands over my heart. "I'm touched. Deeply, deeply touched."

"Let's not get carried away," says Hambone. "Odds are they can't regenerate."

Suddenly, there's a commotion. Loud voices. Footsteps. Somebody screams. A door slams.

"What do you think is going on?" I say.

"Only one way to find out," says Hambone.

He starts down the hallway.

"Wait," I say. But it's too late. He's already gone.

CHAPTER FIFTEEN

STOP! OR I'LL THROW A CAN OF TOMATO SOUP AT YOU!

I take a deep breath and follow close behind Hambone.

"I think it's coming from one of the fourth-grade classrooms," I say. "Maybe even my old room."

The commotion gets louder.

"This way," says Hambone. "And remember to stay close. If it's who I think it is, we'll be better off working together."

I don't want it to be who he thinks it is.

I want it to be cute little pink fluffy bunny rabbits hopping around all nice and happy like. Hippity-hop. Hippity-hop. Isn't the world a wonderful pace?

135

But I know it isn't.

CRASH!

Something flies through the window in front of us, shattering the glass and landing by our feet.

It's a can of tomato soup.

I look in the classroom where it came from.

GULP!

Zombie gorillas! And they've got the Skills and Thrills kids backed up in a corner!

Some of the kids are standing up on the desks, kicking at the zombie gorillas to keep them away. Kenny Martin is one of them. Except he keeps reaching into a bag he has with him on the desk and taking out cans of tomato soup to throw at the zombie gorillas.

(I was just kidding about the bag full of tomato soup cans, by the way. I didn't think that was a real thing. But maybe I'm psychic— you know, have that ESP stuff. That would be cool.)

The zombie gorillas get closer and closer. It doesn't look as if the Skills and Thrills kids will be able to hold them off much longer.

Oh-my-shneggies!

I've never seen somebody get their flesh eaten off before. And I don't think I want to now.

One of the zombie gorillas grabs Kenny Martin by the neck. Kenny tries hitting it on the head with a can of tomato soup. That doesn't work. The zombie gorilla just grunts. Kenny struggles. As he's struggling, he makes eye contact with me. He mouths something. I think he's saying, "Help me!"

Should I? I don't know. I'm kind of in a quandary here.

Now, before you say that I have to help Kenny because human beings have an obligation to help other human beings who are in trouble, and before you say that if I don't help him, I'm a horrible human being—

which I'm not; I'm a nice human being—
let me just say that I haven't mentioned
everything there is to mention about Kenny
Martin. Like he's the biggest bully in the
school. And he bullies me on a daily basis.
Why I failed to mention this is probably
because it's not my favorite thing to talk
about. Obviously.

I think about what I should do.

Is it really a bad thing if the zombie
gorilla eats Kenny's flesh off? I mean, I have
thought of worse things I would like to do to
him. Like this medieval punishment I read
about. I'll spare you the details. Let's just say
it wouldn't be pleasant. Now wouldn't that
be worse for Kenny?

So you see, I'm really trying to look on
the bright side of things. That's how nice I am.

OK. You're right. That's silly. I know. And

I hope you know that I would never subject Kenny to any kind of medieval punishment. It's just the victim in me talking.

Speaking of victims, Kenny is still struggling.

I have to do something. Quick.

I throw my hammer as hard as I can at the zombie gorilla. It hits it in the back. The zombie gorilla drops Kenny and turns around. It grunts at me.

"How'd that work out for you?" says Hambone.

It didn't. Not only did I lose my weapon, but the only thing I accomplished was making the zombie gorilla angry. In fact, I made all of the zombie gorillas angry. Because they all turn around.

"Fasten your seatbelts," says Hambone. *"It's going to be a bumpy fight."*

"Forget that," I say. "Let's get out of here."

The zombie gorillas arrange themselves into rows. One right behind the other.

Uh-oh. I've seen that formation before. They are getting ready to attack.

"Um, Hambone," I say. "You know I'm not great at math. But there's just two of us and we have only one weapon. You know what that equals don't you?"

I don't give Hambone the time to do the math in his head. "Let's get out of here," I say, grabbing him by the collar.

The zombie gorillas chase after us.

Here we go again. But at least they're leaving the Skills and Thrills kids alone now. That's a good thing. So if these zombie gorillas catch up to us and eat our flesh off, at least I can say the last thing I did before I turned into a zombie gorilla was save a bunch of kids who like to make fart sounds in class. Now am I such a horrible human being?

We turn the corner.

Oh-My-Shneggies!

More zombie gorillas. And they're blocking the hallway.

We run into the gym.

Come on, now. Even more zombie gorillas!? What are we going to do?

Luckily, the rope is still hanging from the ceiling. Thank you, gymnastics unit.

"This way," I say. "We'll Tarzan swing over them. It's the only way we can make it to the door."

I grab hold of the rope. "Ahh,

ahahahahahhhh!!!!" I yell, as I pound on my chest.

"Seriously?" says Hambone.

"What?" I say.

"Why do you get to be Tarzan?" he says.

"It's my idea," I say. "But you can stay here if you want."

He doesn't.

He grabs hold of the rope and we run, jump, and swing our way over the heads of the swarming zombie gorillas.

Ahh, ahahahahahhhh!!!!

We land safely and then burst through the door and out onto the playground. Hambone stops and goes back over to the door. He secures his mallet in between the handles so the zombie gorillas can't open it from their side.

Then we run, run, run.

CHAPTER SIXTEEN

KILLER BEES, ZOMBIE GORILLAS, AND BIG, HAIRY GUYS ON HARLEYS

"I'm sick of all this running," says Hambone. He stops by the side of the road and puts his paws on his knees. He's panting like mad.

"You're just out of shape," I say.

"Being out of shape has nothing to do with it," he says. "What's the point of all this running? It's not doing anything for us."

"Let's just take a breather," I say. I put my arms up over my head. It's something our gym teacher, Mr. Rigstein, tells us to do when we're tired from running. "Once we catch our breath, then we can figure out what to do next."

"What to do next?" says Hambone, standing up straight. "I'll tell you what we have to do next: take the fight to those zombie gorillas. We should have done that back at the school."

"That definitely wasn't the time or place and you know that. We're lucky we got out alive."

Just then, I hear a buzzing sound in the distance. Oh, no. That's all we need. Killer bees. Could this day get much worse? But as I keep listening, I notice the buzzing sound changing. It goes from buzzing to growling. That's not killer bees. That's zombie gorillas!

I step into the street to see where they're coming from.

"If this is who I think it is, you know what to do, right?" I say.

"What's that?" says Hambone.

"Run," I say.

Hambone looks at me, frowning.

"Not the time or place again?" he says.

"Do we have any weapons?" I say. "I didn't think so. But if you want to stay, be my guest. Have fun. It was nice knowing you."

"Oh, don't be like that," he says, coming over to me and putting his arm around my shoulder. "You'll miss me if I'm gone."

"Don't think so," I say, shrugging him off. "I'll just go to the pound again and get a new dog."

"I'm just busting your chops," he says. "Why are you getting so mad?"

"Because this is serious," I say. "The fate of the world is on our hands. So stop fooling around and be serious."

"OK, OK," he says. He crosses his arms over his chest, purses his lips, and narrows his eyes.

"What are you doing?" I say.

"This is me being serious."

It doesn't last. Right after Hambone says that, he breaks down laughing.

So much for being serious. I guess you really can't teach an old dog new tricks.

Oh, well. I don't have time to worry about that.

The growling is getting closer.

I bend down and touch my toes. Got

to stretch. Don't want to pull a hammy at a time like this.

"Can you see them yet?" says Hambone.

"Just about," I say. "They're coming around the corner now."

I get myself ready in a good runner's position.

On your mark. Get set.

There they are!

Wait a second.

Those aren't zombie gorillas. It's just a bunch of big, dirty, hairy guys on Harleys. So that was the growling sound—their motorcycles. Phew! I can't tell you how happy I am to see a motorcycle gang. In fact, I don't think I've been happier in all my life.

The lead motorcycle guy stops in front of me and Hambone. He straddles his Harley. It's sparkly pink and purple. Interesting choice of colors. I bet he must be the leader of the gang. He's bigger and dirtier and hairier than the others. He's wearing an American-flag bandana on his head, thick goggles, and a black leather jacket. He also has a goatee and a scar that goes from his right eye across to his right ear. On his left forearm, he's got a tattoo of a German soldier with an X through it. The tattoo looks like he drew it on with a ball-point pen.

"Hey, kid," he says to me. "You seen

any of those Germans around here?"

"Excuse me?" I say.

"Germans?" he says. "Don't you know we're under attack by the Germans? It's like Pearl Harbor all over again."

"I think he's been drinking too much motor oil, if you know what I mean," whispers Hambone.

"Shh," I say. "Stay back and let me handle this."

I turn back to the leader. "Why do you think the Germans are attacking?"

"That's what some crazy old guy said right after he landed his plane practically on top of us," says the leader. "Got out and started screaming that the Germans were coming."

Oh. Now it makes sense.

"That was Mr. Oswalt," I say. "He thinks they're Germans, but they're really zombie gorillas."

"Come again, kid?" says the leader.

"Zombie gorillas," I repeat. "We're being attacked by zombie gorillas."

"Zombie gorillas, you say? Huh?" The leader turns to the rest of his motorcycle gang. "Did you hear that, boys? Now we're after zombie gorillas. What do you think about that?"

The other motorcycle guys cheer, whooping and hollering at the top of their lungs.

"See?" says the leader. "It's all the same to us. But first, I have to do this." He takes a ball-point pen and draws a zombie gorilla on his right forearm. It's really good. Surprisingly accurate.

152

He admires his handiwork a moment, and then he puts an X through it.

"Now we're ready," he says.

"Ready for what?" I say.

"To get us some of these zombie gorillas," says the leader.

Looks like he's about to get his wish. Here come the zombie gorillas knuckle-walking down the street. And they're not getting the funniest looks from everyone they meet. In fact, there's nobody on the street. And even if there were, nobody would think it funny to see zombie gorillas coming.

I know I sure don't.

"Excuse me, sir," I say. "But those zombie gorillas you want are right behind you."

"Hey, thanks, kid," says the leader. "You are now about to witness the strength of the Mama's Boys—the biggest, baddest motorcycle gang on the planet."

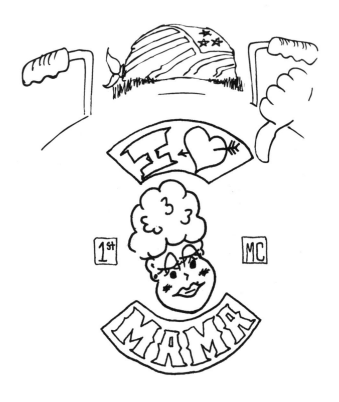

He points to the insignia on the back of his leather jacket. It's a lady's head with the words "I heart Mama" around it.

Then he signals for the rest of his gang to turn their motorcycles around and go after the zombie gorillas. They do.

Time for me and Hambone to exit, stage left!

Chapter Seventeen

Don't Bring a Squirt Gun To
a Zombie Gorilla Fight

"Let's get out of here quick," I say, going over to Hambone. "Before it's too late."

He doesn't budge.

"Come on," I say.

He shakes his head. "No way. I want to see what happens. Mama's Boys versus zombie gorillas. Are you kidding? You can't make this stuff up."

"Do I have to drag you out of here by the collar again?"

"I'd like to see you try. Besides, this is a golden opportunity for us."

"What do you mean?"

"Aren't you forgetting about this?" he says, showing me the can of spray paint. "All we have to do is wait for one of the zombie gorillas to get his brains smashed in by one of the Mama's Boys, and then we can tag it."

Darn him. He's right. We have to do this. But if we do it, we're going to do it from a safe distance.

I tell this to Hambone.

"But we can't be so far away we can't see what's going on," he says. "What good will that do?"

I point to a row of hedges a few feet back from the street. The good thing about them is that they're close enough to the action but also bushy enough that if things get hairy, we can duck behind them for cover.

It's a perfect compromise. So we go

over and settle into our spots.

"By the way," says Hambone. "How stupid is the name Mama's Boys?"

"Pretty stupid," I say. "Definitely doesn't instill fear when you hear it."

"I have a perfect one for your gang," he says.

"Oh, yeah?" I say. "What is it?"

"Sir Peas-A-Lot and His Merry Band of Green Veggies."

"Very funny," I say. "OK. Your turn now. What would you call your motorcycle gang if you had one?"

Hambone thinks. "The Mongrels."

That is awesome.

But I'm not going to tell him that. I won't give him the satisfaction.

Petty? Yes. But he deserves it after the name he gave my gang.

Speaking of gangs, the leader of the Mama's Boys stops his motorcycle in front of the zombie gorillas. He stares them down. Then he takes his pointer finger and drags it across his throat. The zombie gorillas just grunt. Symbolic gestures are lost on them.

Oh, well.

It's go time.

On the leader's signal, the Mama's Boys attack the zombie gorillas. Some crash their motorcycles right into them, while others jump off and bull rush the zombie gorillas, wielding foam swords, rubber bands, jump ropes, and squirt guns.

159

"You've got to be kidding me," I say. "Are these guys for real?"

Hambone howls. "Five bucks says this is over in two minutes."

Maybe not even thirty seconds.

"Ouch, that's got to hurt," I say as a zombie gorilla snatches a squirt gun out of the hands of one of the Mama's Boys and proceeds to repeatedly whack him over the head with it. Over and over until he collapses to the ground in a heap of leather.

Another one pinned underneath his motorcycle acts as a trampoline for two baby zombie gorillas.

"This is getting ugly," says Hambone.

And it is.

Everywhere I look, the zombie gorillas are pummeling the Mama's Boys. They're falling down all over the street. Some are trying desperately to get back on their motorcycles.

No luck.

Zombie gorillas stop them and then proceed to tear into their flesh.

"Now what?" I say.

Miraculously, the leader of the Mama's Boys is still alive. He picks up a jump rope and swings it over his head, gathering momentum for what he does with it next: fling it at the zombie gorilla lunging for him.

"Gotcha," says the leader as the jump rope wraps several times around the zombie gorilla's neck.

He yanks down hard on the jump rope, forcing the zombie gorilla to the ground. Then he spins the zombie gorilla around like a hammer thrower in a track-and-field event. Once the zombie gorilla is elevated high enough off the ground, he releases his grip, sending the zombie gorilla sailing through the air.

It lands by us, head splattering open like an overripe cantaloupe.

"Please resist the urge to eat some," says Hambone.

"Very funny," I say. "Now tag it—quick."

Hambone goes over to the zombie gorilla, but instead of tagging it like I said to do he pretends to take a selfie with it.

"Stop fooling around," I say. "There's no time for that."

And there isn't. Zombie gorillas are everywhere. And before I know it all I can see is a blur of grey fur and yellow fangs.

I'm about to go and check on

Hambone when he suddenly comes crawling back behind the row of hedges.

"Well?" I say.

"I know what you're thinking," he says. "Did I tag the zombie gorilla or didn't I? Well, to tell you the truth, in all this excitement I kind of lost track myself. But since we're talking about zombie gorillas here who can eat your flesh clean off you've got to ask yourself one question: *'Do I feel lucky?' Well, do you, Peas?"* 🎬

"Seriously?" I say. "Now's not the time to quote from *Dirty Hairy.* Did you tag the zombie gorilla or not?"

"Relax," says Hambone. "I put a nice big banana on its back."

"A banana?" I say. "That's original."

"Thank you," says Hambone. "Now let's keep an eye on that zombie gorilla to see if it comes back to life."

Waiting...waiting...

Still dead.

"But I was so sure," I say, shaking my head. "Well, maybe–Whoa! Look at that!"

Shooting through the air like a leather comet is a Mama's Boy. He lands right in front of us.

"Look like anyone you know?" I say.

Hambone growls.

"Aw, come on. That was funny. I mean, a zombie gorilla tossed you the exact same way. Of course, you were in the air longer. On account of you being lighter."

He growls some more.

"What's the matter? You can bust everybody else's chops, but the second somebody does it to you, you get all mad?

That's a little unfair, don't you think?"

More growling.

"Oh, I'm so scared. But you can stop now—I get the point."

But Hambone doesn't stop.

OK. He's going too far now. And I'm going to tell him so.

I look at Hambone.

OH-MY-SHNEGGIES!

That wasn't Hambone growling. That was the zombie gorilla.

The previously-dead-and-tagged-with-a-banana-but-now-back-to-life zombie gorilla.

And it's got Hambone by the throat.

"Stand back," says a voice. It's the leader of the Mama's Boys. He's going to help Hambone. And not a moment too soon.

He jumps on the zombie gorilla's back and yells, "Leave him alone you big meany."

The zombie gorilla staggers backwards, still holding onto Hambone. So the leader thumps it on the head. "I said leave him alone."

This aggravates the zombie gorilla. I think. I don't know. All I know is that it lets go of Hambone and then throws the leader to the ground.

"OK," says the leader, getting up on his feet. "Now get out of here while you still can."

He doesn't have to tell us twice. We hightail it out of there faster than you can say "Kenny Martin is a mama's boy."

Chapter Eighteen
It's The Antidote, Dum-Dum

This isn't good.

This isn't good.

This isn't good.

No. It's terrible.

This is terrible.

This is terrible.

This is terrible.

"What are you babbling about over there?" says Hambone.

"Oh, nothing," I say. "It's only my worst fear has now been realized, that's all."

(Up until this point, my worst fear has been being shrunk to miniature size and then

running from a giant crack opening up in the earth only to fall through that crack, turning everything pitch black and covering me with slime so I can't breathe. But now, right up there at numero uno is zombie gorillas that won't die. Worst fear ever!)

I look around.

Boy, the woods seemed like the perfect place to hide out when Hambone suggested it, but now I'm regretting the move.

It's probably all this talk about worst fears, but it seems that behind every tree, zombie gorillas are lurking. Licking their chops. Salivating over the prospect of more flesh. My flesh. And there's nothing I can do to stop them.

I sit down and bury my face in my hands.

"Are you crying?" says Hambone, jumping down off the rock he's been sitting on and coming over to me. *"There's no crying. There's no crying in zombie gorilla brain smashing!"* 🎬

"I'm not crying," I say, looking up at him. "But how can you not be upset? What are we going to do now?"

"I'm open to any ideas you have," says Hambone.

The trouble is I don't have any. I need to think. Think. Think. Think.

"You have any ideas, yet?" says Hambone.

I shake my head.

"Come on," he says. "You're the expert when it comes to zombies, remember?" he says. "Just think back to all the books you've read. There must be something in one of

169

them that can help."

"That's the problem," I say. "In none of the books I've read have the zombie gorillas come back to life. Once you smash their brains in, they're dead. And they stay dead. This is completely different. It's terrible."

"There has to be something," says Hambone, pacing back and forth. "I'll keep smashing their brains in if I have to. But I'd rather not have to, if you know what I mean."

"I hear what you're saying. But I don't know. I wish I could go up to Evil Doctor Crazy Gorilla and ask him what was in that green potion."

Wait a second.

"That's it," I say.

"What's it?" says Hambone.

"Evil Doctor Crazy Gorilla," I say. "He's

a crazy mad-scientist guy. And it was his green potion that turned the ordinary gorillas into zombie gorillas."

"Yeah, so?" says Hambone.

"So. Forget about about zombies for a second and think about all the science-fiction movies we've seen."

"What about them?"

"Come on–the mad scientists? They don't just make potions they also make antidotes. Just in case something goes terribly wrong."

"That's right," says Hambone, clasping his paws together. "So if we have the antidote we can turn the zombie gorillas back into ordinary gorillas."

"That's how we'll stop them," I say. "Of course, the only question now is how do we get our hands on that antidote?"

Hambone grins from ear to ear.

"I have an idea," he says.

"Great," I say. "What is it?"

"You're going to love it."

Chapter Nineteen

One Bad Idea Deserves Another

The last time Hambone said I was going to love one of his ideas was when he wanted me to play dead on the train tracks. "The look on the conductor's face will be priceless," he said. But I wasn't going to risk my life for a practical joke.

"Are you ready to hear my idea?" says Hambone, smiling.

I brace myself. "Can't wait."

"OK," he says. "You know how I spent all that time in the pound on Kenny Lane?"

"Yeah." That's where I got Hambone. Not the nicest place in the world. You walked in and—bam! Doggie odor. And not the good kind. If there is a good kind.

"And you know the security guard there?" he continues. "The one who sat on his butt all night long when he should have been walking around?"

"Didn't he just watch movies or something?" I say.

"That's the one."

"What about him?"

"Nothing," says Hambone, frowning. "I'd like to forget everything about him. But what I can't forget about is the movie he watched every single night."

"Let me guess," I say. "It was *King Gorilla.*"

Hambone eyes me suspiciously. "Have I told you this before?"

"Not exactly," I say. "I just put it together right now, if you want to know the truth. I knew something happened to you with that movie when you were younger. That's why you hate gorillas, right?"

"Yeah, well, let me tell you," he says, "watching that movie ad nauseam would make anyone a gorilla hater. But that's not the point. The point is the movie holds the key to us finding the antidote."

"How is that possible?" I shrug.

Hambone gives me a knowing look. "The key rhymes with shady."

"Come again?"

"What rhymes with shady?"

"I don't know. I'm not good at rhyming."

"Come on, think," prods Hambone. "Frady? Spady? Zady?"

"Drawing a blank here."

Hambone throws his paws up in disgust. "It's lady."

I still have no idea where this is going.

"What does this have to do with the movie?" I say.

"I'm getting there," says Hambone. "In the movie, there's this lady. Fay. King Gorilla likes Fay. He goes gaga over her and doesn't want anything bad to happen to her, so he takes her to his cave to protect her. Comprende?"

I nod. "Lady. Fay. King Gorilla. Gaga. Cave. Got it."

"Good," says Hambone. "Now gorillas and zombie gorillas are basically the same thing. Same DNA. Which means if a zombie gorilla sees someone that looks like Fay, it's going to want to take her someplace safe where nothing bad can happen to her."

"I guess," I say. "Keep going."

Hambone stares at me. "That's it. That's my idea for finding the antidote."

"I'm sorry," I say. "I must have missed something. What's your idea again?"

"You should dress up like Fay."

I'm stunned. I'm mortified. Bowled over. At a loss. "Me? You want me to dress up like Fay? The lady in the movie?"

"That's right."

"Oh, no."

"Oh, yes."

This can't be happening. Just when you think it can't get any worse than playing dead on the train tracks—now comes this spectacularly bad idea: dressing up like a lady.

"Why don't you do it?" I say. "It's your idea."

"I would, but a zombie gorilla will never buy it," says Hambone. "Me, a lady? Look at my legs—they're all hairy."

I shake my head. "What zombie gorilla would think I was a lady?"

"Are you kidding?" says Hambone, smiling. "Put one of your mother's dresses on you, some jewelry, maybe a little makeup, some rouge, and voila: what zombie gorilla wouldn't think you were a lady?"

I shake my head some more. "You're crazy if you think I'm going to dress up like a lady."

"You have to," says Hambone. "It's the only way we'll ever find the antidote."

"How is my dressing up like a lady

178

going to help us find the antidote?"

Hambone slaps his paw to his face. *"What we've got here is failure to communicate."* ▇ He shakes his head and sighs. "Have you not been listening to a single word I've said? OK. I'll walk you through it again. You dress up like Fay. The zombie gorilla goes gaga over you. He grabs you. He takes you someplace safe."

"I got that part," I say. "But where does finding the antidote come in?"

"I guarantee you the safe place where the zombie gorilla takes you will be Evil Doctor Crazy Gorilla's secret hideout," says Hambone.

"Go on."

"And I also guarantee you that's where we'll find his laboratory with all his potions and stuff. And by stuff I mean the antidote."

179

"What if he's keeping it someplace else?"

"It'll be there."

"And if it isn't?"

"You got any other ideas?"

I don't.

Hambone walks over to me and puts his arm around my shoulder. "I know you have some misgivings about this. Believe me, if I had any other ideas that I thought would work, I'd tell you. But I don't. This is the one. It'll work. It's foolproof."

"Foolproof?" I say.

"That's right," says Hambone, patting me on the chest. "And what's more, just think about what will happen after: we'll be famous. They'll dedicate statues made in our likeness. We'll be known forever as Peas and Hambone: the kids who rid the world of zombie gorillas. Saved the human race. Let freedom ring."

HERO HAMBONE (AND PEAS)

I think I've heard this before.

"And all because of you, Peas, my man," he continues. "All because you had the courage—no, the fortitude—to put aside your doubts and fears and do this." His face softens. "I'm in awe of you. I really am." He starts bowing in front of me. "I bow down to the almighty, Peas. Bow. Bow."

I know he's just messing with me.

Trying to persuade me to dress up like a lady. But it works. "Get up," I say.

"So you'll do it?"

Of course I will. The fate of the world depends upon it.

CHAPTER TWENTY

PEAS LOOKS LIKE A LADY

I'm standing in front of a full-length mirror wearing nothing but my underwear.

"Here. Try this one," says Hambone, handing me another one of my mother's dresses. The first hundred or so he had me try on were either too long or too short, so I'm hoping this one is just right.

I take the dress off the hanger.

Boy, am I glad nobody's home. How embarrassing that would be if my mom and dad walked in on me right now. You know, when my parents said they were going out to eat and I could just heat up some leftovers if I got hungry I was a little mad. But now I couldn't be happier.

I hand the hanger to Hambone and put on the dress.

"So?" says Hambone, grinning. "What do you think?"

"I think you're enjoying this way too much," I say.

"That's beside the point," he says. "So, have we found the one you just absolutely have to have? Is it to die for?" He giggles and puts his paw up to his mouth. "Oops. Bad choice of words."

"You know," I say, smoothing out the dress. "This may come as a big shock to you, but making fun like you are isn't helping."

"Aw, come on," he says. "If I can't have some fun with this, what can I have fun with? I mean, it's not every day my best friend dresses up like a lady. You want me to give up a golden opportunity like this?"

I guess not. "Just keep the jokes to a minimum. OK?"

Hambone makes an X over his heart. "Swear," he says. Then out of the corner of his mouth, he adds, "You're lucky I'm not taking pictures."

"Hey."

"Just kidding."

He'd better be.

I look at myself in the full-length mirror.

This dress definitely fits the best. Wait a second. I mean, it's not like I know how a dress is supposed to fit. Don't get the wrong idea. I've never worn a dress before. I mean, well, yes, maybe, one time I did wear a dress, but it was part of a Halloween costume—I was a wizard. Plus, I was like six or something.

"Turn around," says Hambone, twirling his finger at me. "Let me get a good look at you."

"Seriously?" I say.

"Just do it."

I turn around.

"Wait a second," says Hambone. He walks behind me and tucks in the tag in the back. "There."

"All better now?" I say.

"You can't have a tag showing. That's not very ladylike," he says. He steps to the side and looks at me in the full-length mirror. "So?"

I shrug. "It's good enough, I guess."

"Good enough?" he says. "Do you know what I'm looking at?"

No. And I can't wait to hear.

"I'm looking at the spitting image of Fay," he continues. "Wow. if I didn't know any better, I'd say you were her."

"Very funny," I say.

"No, I'm serious," he says. *(Yeah, right.)* "There's not one zombie gorilla that's going to know the difference. I mean there's no way one of them is going to stop and say, 'Hey, this isn't a lady. This is Peas in a dress.'" He stops and flashes me a mischievous smile. "Hey, that wasn't half bad. Get it. Peas

187

in a dress? Psss!"

He breaks down laughing.

"Oh, so this is funny, huh?" I say. *"Funny how? Like I'm a clown, I amuse you?"* 🎬

Hambone gathers himself together. "Now, now," he says.

"No," I say. "I'll show you funny. I'll take this thing off right now. See how it fits you." I threaten to unzip the dress. "Better start shaving your legs."

"Come on," says Hambone. "I'll give it to you—that last part might have been a little too much. But all joking aside, let's not forget what we're doing this for. The human race is counting on you."

"Fine," I say. "Let's just go before I change my mind."

I start putting on my high heels.

"Wait, wait," says Hambone. "Before we go we need some final touches."

He goes into my mother's dresser and takes out a silver necklace and silver clip-on earrings. He hands them to me.

"Do I have to?" I say.

"Gorillas like silvery things," he says.

I put them on.

Hambone goes into my mother's makeup case and takes out a tube of lipstick.

"Pucker up," he says.

"Do I have to?" I say.

"Human race," he says. "Remember the

human race."

I pucker up.

Boy, this better work. If I do all this and the zombie gorilla just eats my flesh off? What a way to go. And just think, my last memories will be of me standing in my mother's bedroom getting dressed up like a lady. Lipstick and all.

Hambone looks me over. "OK," he says. "I think we're good to go." He steps aside. "After you."

I take a deep breath.

You can do this, I say to myself. You can do this.

CHAPTER TWENTY-ONE

A MATCH MADE IN ZOMBIE GORILLA HEAVEN

What I can't do is walk in high heels.

It goes something like this: Click. Click. Swud!

The clicks are the sound the high heels make hitting the hardwood floor in my mother's bedroom. The swud is the sound I make hitting the hardwood floor in my mother's bedroom.

Ouch!

I rub my butt. If this keeps up, my butt is going to be one giant black-and-blue mark.

I get up.

I steady myself.

"Maybe go slower this time," offers Hambone.

"You think?"

Just then, Hambone lets one rip.

"Hey," I say. *"I'm walking here! I'm walking here!"* 🎬

"So?"

"So, the least you can do is say excuse me."

"Why?"

"Um, you just farted."

"No I didn't."

"You sure did. I heard it."

"It wasn't me. Must have been somebody else."

I turn back around and give him a look. "We're the only ones here."

"It wasn't me," says Hambone, shooing me forward.

Whatever.

Click. Click. Click. Click.

"Atta boy," says Hambone. "Now you're getting the hang of it."

And I am. I get all the way down the stairs and into the living room without falling once. Not too bad if I do say so myself.

I pause at the front door.

"Well, what are you waiting for?" says Hambone impatiently.

"Just give me a second," I say.

I take another deep breath.

Frrrrrtttttttt!

Hambone lets another one rip.

"Again?" I say.

"What?" he says.

"Come on," I say. "Are you going to tell me that wasn't you as well? It sounded like it started rumbling around in your stomach, picked up steam in your intestines, and then growled its way out your butt."

"It wasn't me," he says.

"It's OK to admit you have serious gas issues," I say, turning around to look at him.

OH-MY-SNEGGIES!

Hambone was telling the truth. It wasn't him. The sounds I heard were coming from zombie gorillas. They're in the house!

"Quick!" I yell. "Run!"

"What?" says Hambone, not moving. He doesn't see the zombie gorillas knuckle-

194

walking down the hallway toward him.

I grab Hambone by the collar. "We have to get to the basement," I say, dragging him with me.

Click-click-click-click-click-click-slam!

Phew! That was close!

"I'm sorry I thought you had gas issues," I say as I lean against the basement door. Acting like a barricade.

Hambone throws up his paws.

"What?" I say.

"What are you doing?" he says, looking completely baffled. "You need to open up that door and get out there."

"But there are zombie gorillas out there," I point out.

"Exactly," he says. "They need to see you, or my idea won't work."

195

I shake my head. "I don't know about this."

"What's the matter?" says Hambone.

"I don't know," I say. "But seeing the zombie gorillas, knowing they are just on the other side of this door—it's kind of a bit much. I don't think I can do this. I'm not up for it. I mean, what if he senses that I'm not a lady? Gorillas are pretty smart, you know. What if he says, 'You not lady. You kid in dress. Me not take you anywhere. Me eat your flesh off instead'?"

I start to lose it. Emotionally, I mean. Get a little hysterical.

I'm trembling.

I'm shuddering.

"I can't do this," I blather. "I can't do this. They have fangs. They have fangs. Big yellow fangs. Sharp. Pointy. And they rip.

And they tear. Flesh. Right off your bones. Just ripping and tearing. Tearing and ripping. The agony. The pain. The misery. The woe. Oh, woe is me. Woe is me."

Hambone steps up and slaps me across the face. "Get it together, Peas."

I regain my composure.

"Thank you," I say. "I needed that. I really did. Wow. I lost my head for a second there."

"Well find it again," says Hambone. "The whole world needs you. And your head."

I take a deep breath.

"I got it," I say. "I'm good. Good to go."

I open the basement door but then close it back up again real quick.

"So you really think this is going to

work?" I say.

"Trust me."

Yeah, that's a good one. The same kid who said to it was safe to jump out of a tree with a sled. Go slaloming down the snow bank. Right into oncoming traffic. Yeah. That was safe.

Oh, shneggies. What have I gotten myself into?

"Do I have to count to three?" says Hambone.

"No," I say. "I'm going to do this."

"So do it already—while we're young."

OK. This really is it. No more wavering. No more dithering. Just be brave.

I summon the courage.

I open the basement door.

Click. Click. Click. Click.

"Oh, look at me," I say, using my best impersonation of a lady's voice. "I'm just a lady out walking by myself. That's right. Lady here. Not a kid in a dress and silver earrings and a silver necklace and high heels and lipstick. Nope. One hundred percent lady."

"Wow," says Hambone, calling out

from behind the basement door. "Very convincing. You're probably going to have to beat the zombie gorillas off with a stick."

Very funny. I'd like to see him do better.

Just then, a zombie gorilla knuckle-walks up to me.

"Hey, you're kind of cute," I say. *(Don't ask me why. It just sounded like something I should say.)*

The zombie gorilla stares at me.

I stare back.

Can you say awkward?

As it stares at me, the zombie gorilla lowers its eyebrows and curls its lips back, exposing every inch of his big, yellow fangs.

This isn't good. It's not buying it. Not for one second.

What was I thinking agreeing to this

idea? Stupidest idea ever!

Drool pours out of the corners of the zombie gorilla's mouth. It reminds me of Carl Spagano. He's this kid at my school. A fifth grader. Big oaf. Drools all the time. Should start calling him "zombie gorilla boy." Hey, that's kind of funny. I'll have to tell Hambone that one. If I make it out of this alive.

The zombie gorilla starts pounding its chest and whooping.

I brace myself.

One of two things is about to happen in the next five seconds. Either Hambone's plan works, or the zombie gorilla eats my flesh.

I sure hope it's the first one.

The zombie gorilla lunges out and grabs me. Wraps me up in its arms. Tight.

He stares at my eyes.

He stares at my lips.

Does he want to....?

Please don't kiss me! Please don't kiss me! Eat my flesh off instead. That's much better.

Wait! What am I saying? This is crazy. This is crazy.

I'm feeling faint. The world around me gets darker. Like somebody turning the lights off one by one. Good-bye, cruel world. It's getting darker and darker. And then: all the lights go off.

203

Chapter Twenty-Two

Best Laid Plans Of Dogs And Ladies

I come to.

Wow.

So that's what fainting is like. Huh. Have to say, not a big fan. But I guess I shouldn't complain. It's better than what could have happened: that zombie gorilla kissing me.

I look around.

This place is...um...what's the word I'm looking for? Um? How about dirty? No. Creepy? No. Cavey? No. Gloomy? No. Spidery? No. Spider-cobwebery? Is that even a word? Maybe I need more than one word. Maybe the best way to describe this place is dirty-creepy-cavey-gloomy-spider-cobwebery.

Not sure that does it. Not sure there are enough words in the dictionary to describe where I am. But you get the point—it's not a pleasant place.

So I'm getting out of here.

Oh, great.

The door is locked. So now I'm being treated like a common criminal? That's not very cool. Let's add a new descriptive word to this place: dungeony.

I grab hold of the bars and yank.

Nothing doing.

Uh-oh.

I hear footsteps. Someone is coming.

Hide. Hide. I have to hide. But where? Unfortunately, there isn't anything in here but me.

What to do? What to do?

I stand really still. Maybe whoever is coming won't see me.

This is ridiculous. Who am I kidding? I'm wearing a dress, silver earrings, a silver necklace, high heels, and lipstick. Who isn't going to see that?

I decide to hide in the corner, curling up into a ball and covering my face with my hands. Again, not going to make me invisible, but it's my best option under the circumstances.

Keys jangle.

A lock turns.

The door opens.

It's Hambone.

"Hey," he says. "See? Didn't I tell you this was going to work? Talk about nailing it. Come on, get up. Give me a high five. I deserve a little congratulations here. What an idea." He pauses, lost in thought. "That could be the title of the book they write about us: *Hambone's Amazing, Incredible, Spectacularly Awesome Idea to Save the World from Flesh-Eating Zombie Gorillas.* Yeah. That about sums it up."

"Really?" I say, getting up off the floor. "That's what you're calling it? How about we call it *How Hambone Got His Best Friend to Dress Up Like a Lady and Get Carried Away by a Flesh-Eating Zombie Gorilla?* And let's not forget the sequel: *Where am I?*"

"Relax," says Hambone. "We're exactly where we want to be: Evil Doctor Crazy Gorilla's secret hideout."

"That's supposed to make me feel better?" I say.

"It should."

"Well, it doesn't," I say, straightening out my dress. "So where is this secret hideout, anyway?"

"Take a guess."

"Just tell me," I say. I'm not in the mood to guess.

"Come on," says Hambone. "What's the fun it that? Take a guess."

"No."

"Fine," Hambone sniffs. "Be a baby. Take all the fun out of me telling you we're underneath the Gorilla Kingdom."

"Underneath? Surely you can't be serious."

Hambone does a double take. *"I am serious...and don't call me Shirley."*

Didn't mean to give him such an

easy pitch to hit. But at least it brightens Hambone's mood.

"But yeah," he says. "Underneath. How cool is that?"

"Pretty cool," I say.

"Right?" he says. "I had no idea. So when we got to the Gorilla Kingdom, I was all like, oh, no! Kind of bummed because I was so sure my idea was going to work. But then the zombie gorilla jumped up on the fallen log and yanked on this tree branch sticking out. But it's not a tree branch—it's a lever that looks like a tree branch—and all of a sudden, this rock slid out of the way, and there's this tunnel, and the zombie gorilla just went right in and climbed down, and here we are."

"Great," I say. "I'm glad it all worked out so well in the end."

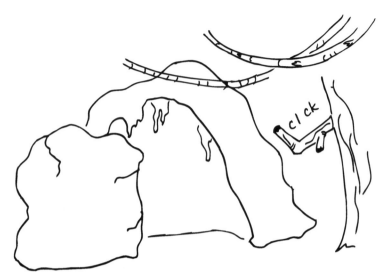

"Come on," says Hambone. "Don't be all Mr. Grumpypants." He stops. He thinks. Then he flashes me a mischievous smile. "Um, I mean, that is, don't be all Mrs. Grumpypants." He starts laughing. "Aw, who am I kidding? Who's going to marry you? You're one ugly lady." He breaks down laughing.

"Now is not the time for busting chops," I say, a little annoyed.

"You're right," he says. "Because what we have to do now is find the antidote. So let's go do that."

"OK," I say. "But before we do do that—"

"That's a lot of do-do."

I give Hambone a look. "Very funny," I say. "Before we do that, tell me something: Where did you get the key?"

"You mean this one?" says Hambone, holding up the key for inspection. "All I had to do was follow that zombie gorilla after it locked you in here. Took me right to  this room that turned out to be Evil Doctor Crazy Gorilla's laboratory. Score! He was asleep. Probably tired out from doing his mad-scientist stuff. So the zombie gorilla put the key on a hook and went to sleep too.

I tiptoed over and grabbed it. Simple."

"You've seen Evil Doctor Crazy Gorilla's laboratory?" I say.

Hambone nods.

"Is the antidote there?" I say.

Hambone nods again.

Wow. I can't believe it. His plan really did work.

I congratulate Hambone.

"All right, then," he says, slapping his paws together. "Time is a wasting. Let's go get us some antidote." He turns and points at the door. "Follow me. This way to Evil Doctor Crazy Gorilla's laboratory."

CHAPTER TWENTY-THREE

SCENT OF A ZOMBIE GORILLA

Tunnels. Tunnels. And more tunnels.

"Are you sure you know where you're going, Hambone?" I say, stopping to catch my breath. "It feels like we've been going around in circles."

"I hate to admit it," says Hambone, "but I didn't really pay any attention when I followed that zombie gorilla. I figured I could always find it again with my nose if I had to."

"So what's the problem?"

Hambone sniffs the air. "Do you smell that?"

213

"You're asking me?" I say. "That's kind of funny, isn't it? You know your sense of smell is about a million times better than mine."

"No, I know. But do you smell that?"

I take a whiff. "I actually don't smell anything," I say. "Is that what happens when you faint—you lose your sense of smell?"

"Well, if you do, it's a good thing because that means you can't smell the stench of zombie gorilla," says Hambone. "That's what I smell. Pee-yew! Can't get it out of my nostrils. And it's not getting any stronger, which isn't good."

"Why not?" I say.

"Because that's how I know I'm getting closer—the scent gets stronger," says Hambone. "But this, this is like a constant stench—it doesn't get stronger or weaker—it just stays the same. I don't understand it."

"Maybe being underground does something to your sense of smell," I say.

"I don't know," says Hambone. He starts sniffing. "This is weird." He keeps sniffing. "It's like…" He comes right up to me, still sniffing. "Whoa," he says, putting his paws up in alarm. "There we go. Now I got it."

"Got what?"

"No wonder I'm thrown off here," he says, putting his nose to my dress and sniffing deeply. "You reek of zombie gorilla."

"I do?" I say, sniffing my dress. "Great. What I always wanted."

"I'll tell you what I want," says Hambone. "I want you to stand about forty feet behind me." He shoos me away from him. "That's right. Keep going. The farther behind the better. That way I won't be smelling you the whole time. Perfect."

I'm standing about forty feet behind him.

"How you doing back there?" says Hambone, smiling reassuringly. "Now don't worry. I'll wait for you before I do anything."

He starts walking down the tunnel.

Before I know it, he's standing outside the door to Evil Doctor Crazy Gorilla's laboratory.

"What's the plan?" I say, catching up to him.

"What do you mean, what's the plan?" says Hambone, giving me a look. "The plan is we go in there and get the antidote."

"Just like that?" I say.

"Yeah," he says. "Just like that. We are on a mission here, you know. A mission to save the world. And we're so close I can taste it."

Hambone looks me in the eyes. "On the count of three: one—two—three!"

CHAPTER TWENTY-FOUR

HERE WE COME TO SAVE THE DAY!

We burst into Evil Doctor Crazy Gorilla's
laboratory.

What the...?

Evil Doctor Crazy Gorilla is nowhere to
be seen. The only thing to be seen is all his

laboratory stuff. On a table are beakers and test tubes filled with all different colored liquids: red and green and yellow and pink and blue. There's smoke billowing out of them. Like lava. Wires and plugs and other contraptions hang from the ceiling. As if someone spent hours sticking them up there. On another table are dissecting tools: knives, scalpels, pliers, razor blades. A bottle with a stopper sits on the table as well. As does a big bowl.

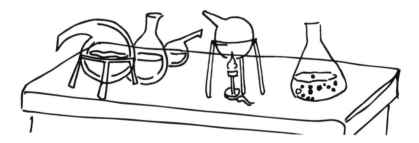

There's more, but I don't have time to tell you about it. Because someone is coming.

Me and Hambone duck behind the door.

Just then, in walks Evil Doctor Crazy Gorilla and the zombie gorilla that took me. They go over to the table with the beakers and test tubes.

Hambone slams the door shut.

The sound startles Evil Doctor Crazy Gorilla. He looks over at us. "What's going on here?" he says. He doesn't wait for us to answer. Instead, he looks directly at me. "How did you escape?"

"I let him out," says Hambone.

"You?" says Evil Doctor Crazy Gorilla. "Who are you?"

"I'm the kid who's going to unleash some Dog Fu on you if you don't hand over the antidote," says Hambone, smirking.

"You're a kid?" says Evil Doctor Crazy Gorilla, looking perplexed. "You look like a dog to me. What's your name? Poochy Poo?"

"They call me Mister Hambone!" snaps Hambone. 🎬

I jump in. "Well, he's not a dog, but a kid; even though he doesn't look like a kid, he looks like a dog. But he shouldn't be a kid right now—he should be a dog." I go over to Hambone and slap him on the nose. "Bad dog. Bad, bad dog."

Hambone pushes me away. "Get out of here, Peas. It's not like it matters. Even if he said a word, do you think they'd believe him? No. He's Evil Doctor Crazy Gorilla. Who'd believe anybody with that name."

Evil Doctor Crazy Gorilla looks at Hambone. "So if you're a dog that's a kid, what's he?" He points at me.

"What does it look like?" says Hambone. "He's a kid dressed like a lady."

"Is this a joke?" says Evil Doctor Crazy Gorilla, looking around. "Am I on one of those hidden-camera shows? Is somebody going to jump out any second and say, 'Smile!'?" He keeps looking around. "So where are the cameras?"

"There aren't any cameras, you crazy weirdo," says Hambone. "There's just us: Peas and Hambone. So you'd better hand over that antidote. I'm not going to ask you again."

Evil Doctor Crazy Gorilla picks up a test tube filled with red liquid. "You mean this antidote?" he says, holding the test tube out to us and then pulling it back right away. "Is this the one you mean? This one?" He holds it out to us again and then pulls it right back. Again.

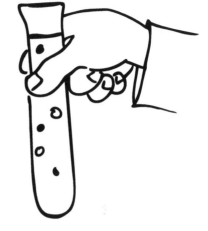

"Is he mocking me?" says Hambone, turning to me.

"Yup," I say.

"He's mocking me. Unbelievable." Hambone turns back toward Evil Doctor Crazy Gorilla. "If you don't give that to me, I'm going to take it."

Evil Doctor Crazy Gorilla laughs. "I'd like to see you try."

Hambone takes a step forward.

GRRRR!

The zombie gorilla beats his chest and then starts knuckle-walking toward Hambone.

Hambone pauses. I think he knows he's in trouble. He doesn't have a weapon. At least not one he can reach from where he's standing.

Luckily, Evil Doctor Crazy Gorilla puts out his arm and stops the zombie gorilla from going after Hambone. He whispers something in its ear. Probably more of that gorilla-whisperer stuff.

The zombie gorilla turns and looks at Hambone. It hoots at him. Like it's telling Hambone that he's lucky it didn't have the chance to go at him. And he might not be so lucky the next time. Then it goes over into the corner and sits down.

I look over at Hambone. He smiles. "He just made it that much easier for me," he says, winking at me. "Ready or not, here I come."

He starts running for Evil Doctor Crazy Gorilla.

But before he can get to him the zombie gorilla jumps up and grabs Hambone by the neck.

"Take your stinking paws off of me you darn dirty zombie gorilla!" yells Hambone. 🎬

Evil Doctor Crazy Gorilla nods at the zombie gorilla. It releases Hambone. Who falls to the ground.

"That was a mistake," says Hambone, getting up and rubbing his neck.

He goes after Evil Doctor Crazy Gorilla again.

This time, when Hambone is within arms reach, Evil Doctor Crazy Gorilla presses a button on the table. A metal cage drops from the ceiling, landing directly on top of Hambone. He's trapped.

"Let me out of here," he says, shaking the bars.

It's no use. He gives up.

"Well," says Hambone, looking at me, "what are you waiting for? Go get him!"

I start. I stop. I hesitate. What other diabolical trap does Evil Doctor Crazy Gorilla have up his sleeve?

Turns out I don't have to do anything to find out.

Evil Doctor Crazy Gorilla pushes another button on the table. A column of smoke rises from the ground. It swirls around me, wrapping me in a cloudy straitjacket.

Uh-Oh!

This can't be good.

CLICK!

227

CHAPTER TWENTY-FIVE

THE ADVENTURES OF CHICKEN BOY

I try not to breathe the smoke, but I can't help it.

Evil Doctor Crazy Gorilla comes over to me. He grabs my hand and leads me across the laboratory.

"Where are we going?" I think I say. I'm not sure. I can't see clearly. I can't even think clearly.

"Just relax, kid," I hear Evil Doctor Crazy Gorilla saying. Or did I?

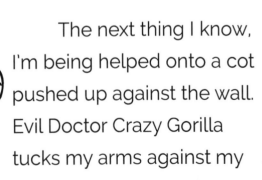

The next thing I know, I'm being helped onto a cot pushed up against the wall. Evil Doctor Crazy Gorilla tucks my arms against my

228

sides and turns my hands palm up. Then he spreads my legs apart so that my feet touch the corners of the cot.

"All of this will be over very soon," says Evil Doctor Crazy Gorilla.

This time I know I heard that. The cloud is suddenly lifting. I can see clearly again. And think clearly again.

"What's going on?" I say. "What was that stuff?"

"Just something I created," he says. "It momentarily incapacitates people. Makes it easier for me to get them to do whatever I want them to do. Especially if it's against their will."

Against their will? What does that mean?

Uh-oh. I know what that means.

I try to move my arms but can't—they're strapped against the cot. Same goes for my feet. And it feels like the more I struggle, the tighter the straps get.

"Now, now," says Evil Doctor Crazy Gorilla. "Don't worry. Just relax and leave the rest to me."

He steps behind me and straps my head down.

Just then I hear a whirling noise followed by a series of beeps. Where's it coming from?

Oh-my-shneggies!

Now I know. Lowering down from the ceiling is a wire with a syringe attached. The syringe stops inches from my face. I can see that it is filled with the same green potion Evil Doctor Crazy Gorilla gave the gorillas in the clearing.

More strange noises and beeps.

This time two small boxes open in the wall above me. Then a mechanical hand slides out from each box. They reach down and grab hold of my mouth, prying it open like a pistachio nut.

No! No! No! I get what's going on. Evil Doctor Crazy Gorilla is going to give me some of the green potion. He wants to turn me into a zombie! But what if it doesn't work? Maybe it only turns gorillas into zombies. Maybe it turns kids into chicken boys. I don't want to be a chicken boy.

"Thaawww! Leazzze! Thaawww!" I'm trying to say, "Stop! Please! Stop!" But under the circumstances it's the best I can do. But who am I kidding? He's not going to stop.

"Don't do it," says Hambone. "I'm warning you."

"Really?" says Evil Doctor Crazy Gorilla. "You're warning me? Says the little doggie—oh, wait. You're not a little doggie. You're a little kid who looks like a little doggie. That's right. My mistake. Let me try it again. Says the little kid who looks like a little doggie—in a cage."

"Not for long," says Hambone. "You'd better be afraid. Be very, very afraid. I'm almost out of here. And when I'm out, I have some Dog Fu with you name on it."

Evil Doctor Crazy Gorilla cackles. "You don't get it," he says. "It's over! I win! You lose! Ha! Ha! Ha! You think you can mess with me? I don't think so! I own you! And soon I'm going to own the world! It'll be mine! All mine! And there's nothing you or anybody else can do to stop me!"

"Wow, somebody sure has an overinflated sense of himself," says

Hambone. "But I guess if you're trying to eliminate the human race and replace it with zombie gorillas, your elevator doesn't go all the way to the top, if you know what I'm saying. You're a few fries short of a Happy Meal. You're not the brightest crayon in the box. You're one spring short of a slinky. You're a few peas short of a casserole. No offense, Peas."

None taken.

"You think I'm crazy?" says Evil Doctor Crazy Gorilla. "I'd like you to know that I have one of the finest scientific minds of my generation. But enough talk. The time for talking is over."

Evil Doctor Crazy Gorilla comes up to the cot. He stands over me. "I don't really know if you are going to turn into a zombie. I've never tested this on human beings before, but what the heck. Whatever happens, happens, right?"

I try to speak again.

"What was that?" says Evil Doctor Crazy Gorilla, putting his hand to his ear. "Did you say something?" He presses a button, and the two hands let go of my mouth. "Speak now, or forever hold your peace."

"Hey, wait a second," I say. "You say you have a great scientific mind? Then you'd know that it isn't ethical to conduct a blind experiment on a human being. It's against the oath all scientists have to take. I know. I'm going to be a scientist someday. But you obviously don't know. So you must not be a real scientist. You're just a fake."

I'm just making this stuff up, totally winging it, but I figure it's worth a shot. What have I got to lose?

"How do you know about the oath?"

says Evil Doctor Crazy Gorilla.

"There is such a thing?" I say.

"No," he says. "Now say ahhh."

Evil Doctor Crazy Gorilla reaches up for the syringe.

I close my eyes.

What a way to go. If I could shake my head in disbelief, I would.

Just then, I see something moving toward me out of the corner of my eye. It's Hambone. Somehow he got out. And now he's sneaking up behind Evil Doctor Crazy Gorilla.

WHUMP!

Hambone wallops Evil Doctor Crazy Gorilla right in the back of the head, knocking him out cold.

236

"How does that Dog Fu taste?" says Hambone, raising his arms in victory.

GRRRR!

Uh-oh.

Can you say angry zombie gorilla? Judging by the look on its face, it didn't care too much for that Dog Fu Hambone unleashed on Evil Doctor Crazy Gorilla.

"Quick," I say. "Press the button on the table."

Hambone presses the button. Smoke rises up and covers the zombie gorilla. Momentarily incapacitating it.

"Now what?" says Hambone.

"Get me out of here," I say.

He does.

"Not so fast," says Evil Doctor Crazy Gorilla, getting up groggily. He staggers over to the wall and pulls a lever.

Uh-oh.

Schlik! Thwump!

I look at Hambone.

238

He looks at me.

We both look down at the floor.

OH-MY–

A trapdoor opens.

–SNEGGIEEEEEEEEEEEES!

We fall...fall....fall...

This isn't going to end well.

Chapter Twenty-Six

Deja Vu!

Thud!

Wow, that wasn't as bad as I thought it was going to be. I'm not saying it was fun to fall ten feet through a trapdoor but the ground isn't as hard as I thought it would be. In fact, it's kind of cushiony.

And hairy?

"You can get off me now," says Hambone.

Oh, so that's why.

Hambone pushes me away and stands up. "I think one of your high heels punctured my lung," he says, rubbing his side. He looks around. "Where are we?"

What the...?

I know where we are.

"Don't you recognize it?" I say, slumping my shoulders in disappointment. "This is the dirty-creepy-cavey-gloomy-spider-cobwebery-dugeony place I was locked up in."

"Oh, yeah, you're right," says Hambone. "Hmm. Pretty sneaky Evil Doctor Crazy Gorilla. Pretty sneaky."

"Pretty sneaky?" I say, sounding a little peeved. "Are you kidding me?"

"Now, now," says Hambone, coming over to me. "Settle down."

"I will most definitely not settle down," I say, pushing him away.

I go to the door and shake the bars. *"I'm mad as hangry elephants longing for lollipops and I'm not going to take it anymore."* 🎬

"Wow, I've never seen this side of you before Peas," says Hambone, smiling. "I like it. Very edgy. And dark. You can join The Mongrels anytime."

"Hardy ha ha."

"But seriously," he continues. "I think it's good you getting angry. To be honest, up until now it has kind of felt like your heart hasn't been in it."

"Yeah, well, enough is enough. I'm all in now."

"You hear that, Evil Doctor Crazy Gorilla?" says Hambone, calling out. "You better get ready. Because Peas and Hambone are coming for you."

"That's what I'm talking about," I say, jumping up and heading toward the door.

"The only trouble is how are we going to get out of this place." I give the bars a good shake. Nothing. I turn back toward Hambone. "You don't still have the key on you by any chance?"

"I wish," he says.

"Let me think." I start to pace back and forth. "There's got to be another way out."

Click. Click. Stop.

I stare at the door.

Why not?

I bend over and touch my toes. I reach from side to side. I take a couple deep breaths. I run in place.

Hambone sits there watching me blankly. "Warming up in case the coach puts you in the big game?" he says. "Or do you just feel like doing a little jazzercise?"

"Just watch," I say.

I get set in a runner's stance and then go for it.

Click. Click. Click. Click. Click. Click.

CLANK!

Thud!

That's going to leave a mark.

Hambone comes over to me. "So that was your bright idea—to break down the door?" he says, shaking his head. "Did you take a sip of dum-dum juice when I wasn't looking?"

I sigh. "So much for being all in," I say, rubbing my shoulder. "I guess maybe it's not meant to be."

GRRRR!

What the...?

OH-MY-SHNEGGIES!

As if it couldn't get any worse, now that zombie gorilla is coming back! It knuckle walks up to the door, crosses his arms and then turns his back to us.

"Great," I say. "Now we have a guard watching us."

Hambone goes over and stares intently at the zombie gorilla.

"What?" I say.

"I don't know why I didn't see it before," he says. "But I think this is the gorilla who threw dirt on me."

"Get out of here."

"No. I'm telling you. It's him."

"Are you sure?"

Hambone studies the zombie gorilla some more.

245

"Yup. Positive."

I go over and take a look for myself. To be honest I don't really remember which gorilla threw dirt on him.

I guess it could be the one. Maybe. But I'll tell you what I am certain about. I'm certain it's holding the key to the door!

I get on my hands and knees and commando crawl over to the door. I reach up. Slowly. Slowly. Don't want the zombie gorilla to notice what I'm doing. Almost there...

"Look what I got," I say, standing up and showing the key to Hambone.

Splsssssssssssssssshhhhhhh gurgle gurgle gurgle.

"What was that?" I say, looking up at the ceiling.

"Sounds like a toilet flushing," says Hambone.

"You know what that means don't you?" I say.

Hambone raises an eyebrow. "Evil Doctor Crazy Gorilla had to go potty?"

"It means he's getting rid of the antidote," I say. "We have to hurry and stop him."

I unlock the door.

GRRRR!

The zombie gorilla blocks our way. Well, duh! Of course he was going to do that. What was I thinking? Now what?

"Stand back," says Hambone, stepping in front of me. "I've been waiting for this moment for a whole year."

He gets set in a Dog Fu stance.

247

I'm about to remind him—

"Hwaieeeee-YAAHHHHHH."

POWIE!

PLOP!

Ouch! Too late.

"I told you Dog Fu has no effect on a zombie gorilla," I say, looking down at Hambone. Hmm. He doesn't look too good. "Are you okay?"

"Hey," he says. "Look at the pretty little lady doggies."

Uh, oh. You know what that means don't you? Starts with a d and ends with azed.

I help Hambone to his feet. "How many

248

fingers am I holding up?" I say.

Hambone shakes it off. "Will you get out of here with that. I'm fine. *It's just a flesh wound.*" 🎬

"Yeah, well, it's going to be all of your flesh if we don't think of something fast," I say. "Look!"

The zombie gorilla knuckle walks in and locks the door.

We're trapped! Gulp!

Is this the end?

I close my eyes.

I open my eyes.

"What's it waiting for?" I say.

"Maybe it's too dumb to know what to do next," says Hambone.

"Um, eat flesh," I say. "That's what

zombies do."

Wait a second. Maybe it doesn't want to do that. Maybe it doesn't want to be a zombie at all.

That's it.

"What are you doing?" says Hambone.

"Getting us out of here," I say, going over to the zombie gorilla. I look in its eyes. "I know how hard this must be for you. You didn't ask for this. If it was up to you you'd be back in the Gorilla Kingdom laughing and throwing dirt with your friends. Am I right? I know I am. What you are now—it's not natural. Gorillas turned into zombies? Talk about messing with the animal kingdom. That's not right. I mean, come on, what's going to happen next? *Dogs and cats living together?*" 🎬

"What?!" says Hambone. "If you

think I would ever sing 'Kumbaya' with Fluffylufugus you're out of your mind."

I ignore Hambone.

"Don't you see," I continue. "You're meant to be a gorilla. Not a zombie. And we can help you. There's an antidote. And we can get it. All you have to do is let us out of here. Then you'll be back laughing and throwing dirt in the Gorilla Kingdom before you know it. So what do you say? Don't you want to be an ordinary gorilla again?"

It works.

The zombie gorilla lets us go.

"Quick," I say, gesturing to Hambone to follow me. "To Evil Doctor Crazy Gorilla's laboratory to get the antidote."

Splssssssssssssssshhhhhhh gurgle gurgle gurgle.

Uh-oh.

I hope it's not too late.

CHAPTER TWENTY-SEVEN

WHO YA GONNA CALL?
PEAS AND HAMBONE!

The door to Evil Doctor Crazy Gorilla's laboratory is locked.

No worries.

I lower my shoulder.

Click. Click. Click. Click. Click. Click. SMASH!

Broke it down in one try!

How do you like me now Evil Doctor Crazy Gorilla!

Um...Evil Doctor Crazy Gorilla?

The laboratory is empty.

Splsssssssssssssshhhhhhh gurgle

gurgle gurgle.

Noooooo! Say it ain't so! Say the human race didn't just get flushed down the toilet.

Suddenly, a door opens.

"Whoa! Do not go in there," says Evil Doctor Crazy Gorilla, fanning the door back and forth. "Something I ate is definitely not agreeing with me."

That's for sure.

Oh, the horror!

No.

Oh, the smell!

But wait a second. You know what that means don't you? Evil Doctor Crazy Gorilla wasn't flushing away the antidote. We still have a chance!

"Hey," says Evil Doctor Crazy Gorilla,

noticing me and Hambone standing there. "How did you two escape?"

"Never mind that," I say. "Hand over the antidote. And do it quickly if you know what's good for you."

"Wow," says Evil Doctor Crazy Gorilla. "For a kid wearing a dress you sure do act tough. Look at me. I'm so scared."

"Just give it to us," I say, ignoring his sarcasm.

Evil Doctor Crazy Gorilla walks over to a table and picks up a test tube filled with red liquid. "You mean this antidote?" he says, holding the test tube out to us and then pulling it back right away. "Is this the one you mean? This one?" He holds it out to us again and then pulls it right back. Again.

Seriously? Didn't we already go through this once before?

"I'm done playing around with you," I say, taking a step forward. "Now be a good little Evil Doctor Crazy Gorilla and give it here." I hold out my hand.

Evil Doctor Crazy Gorilla laughs. "You think you can get this from me?"

"Look around," I say, still holding out my hand. "That zombie gorilla isn't around to help you and we know all of your tricks."

"Do you?" says Evil Doctor Crazy Gorilla, smiling. "Well, what if I do this?"

He pretends to drop the test tube on the floor.

"I'm warning you," I say.

"Or this?" He pretends to dump the red liquid on the floor.

"I'm going to count to three," I say.

Evil Doctor Crazy Gorilla nonchalantly

tosses the test tube from hand to hand.

"One!" I say.

He nonchalantly passes the test tube around his back.

"Two!" I say.

He nonchalantly passes it back and forth under his legs.

"Three!"

I lunge.

Evil Doctor Crazy Gorilla laughs and then nonchalantly steps out of the way.

Thunk!

No. That's not the sound of me hitting the table.

That's the sound of Evil Doctor Crazy Gorilla's head hitting the floor.

Oh, no!

Not only did he slip and fall but he also lost his grip on the test tube. It flies a few inches higher in the air and then starts to come down.

I dive for it. Catching it just before it hits the floor.

Phew!

"That was close," says Hambone, coming over to me.

"You can say that again," I say, getting up off the floor.

We stand there looking down at Evil Doctor Crazy Gorilla.

Hambone pats me on the back. "I knew you had it in you," he says.

"I'm glad you did," I say. "I wasn't so sure. And I'll tell you another thing I'm not sure about—what Evil Doctor Crazy Gorilla slipped on."

"I'll tell you what he slipped on," says Hambone, reaching down and removing a piece of toilet paper stuck to Evil Doctor Crazy Gorilla's shoe. "This!"

Seriously?

"Good thing he's not a strong wiper, huh?" says Hambone, howling.

We continue to stare at Evil Doctor Crazy Gorilla.

"You know something," I say. "I've been meaning to ask you. How did you get out of that cage earlier?"

"I dug a hole."

"Really?"

"Well, I am kind of an expert at digging holes," he says. "But if you want to know the truth, I kind of owe it all to you."

"To me?" I say, taken aback.

"Yeah," he says. "If it weren't for you going on and on and on with that scientist gibberish, I never would have gotten out in time. That bought me the precious extra seconds I needed."

"Glad my desperate bid to save myself from being turned into a zombie could be used to your advantage." Since you can't tell, my tongue is firmly in my cheek when I say that.

Hambone doesn't have a clue. It goes right over his head.

"OW! Ow, ow, ow."

Speaking of heads, Evil Doctor Crazy Gorilla is rubbing the back of his head and attempting to get up.

I wonder if he's seeing little zombie gorillas circling around his head.

Snap out of it, Peas. Focus on Evil Doctor Crazy Gorilla.

Me and Hambone help him get to his feet. In fact, we help him right off his feet and onto the cot he put me on.

"What are you doing?" he asks.

"There, there," I say. "Don't you worry your little head about it. Just leave it to me."

I strap him down the way he did to me.

I look at Hambone. He looks at me.

"That's how we do it!" he says.

We give each other jumping high fives.

We did it!

We stopped Evil Doctor Crazy Gorilla!!

We saved the world!!!

It's good to be Peas and Hambone!!!!

Epilogue

We handed the antidote over to the proper authorities.

They thanked us. They thanked us a lot. In fact, they thanked us so much they said the only proper way to thank us was to give us a reward. After all, we did save the human race.

Hambone kept elbowing me in the side as we waited to hear what our reward was, whispering to me to hold my breath because it was going to be huge.

I told him to stop whispering. I didn't want any of the proper authorities to know that he's not a dog but a kid even though he doesn't look like a kid, he looks like a dog. It probably would not have gone over so well.

But Hambone kept at it. He kept

whispering that I should hold my breath.

Don't hold your breath. It wasn't huge. Just the opposite.

How unhuge? Well, it wasn't statues made in our likeness. Not diamonds. Not Lamborghinis. Not even cold, hard cash. None of that.

Are you ready for what they did give us?

Here goes: a lifetime membership to the zoo.

Swear. That's what they gave us.

I didn't think it was that bad.

Hambone, of course, was so upset

he nearly had a seizure.

You ever try to give CPR to a dog? Me neither.

I had to think of something to calm him down. So I reminded him how much we like the zoo. And so, since we now have this membership, we should at least go back and thank that gorilla who threw dirt on him. After all, he did help us.

Hambone agreed—reluctantly. And I mean very reluctantly. I had to drag him kicking and barking all the way there. Talk about a doggy fit.

Once we got to the zoo, it wasn't much better. He was still kicking and barking. So I had to tell him if he didn't stop, I was going to chain him up in the Gorilla Kingdom. He could live with the gorillas for all I cared.

That did it.

He settled down. And I have to say he did a nice job of saying thanks. He called out to the gorilla in the clearing and told him how much he appreciated everything he did. He also told him that he never truly wanted to unleash Dog Fu on him–it was just his anger talking. And from now on we should all be friends. Then he started singing Kumbaya at the top of his lungs.

It was priceless. I wish I had a video camera so I could put it up on WeTube. We may not have become famous for saving the world from Evil Doctor Crazy Gorilla and his army of zombie gorillas, but once that video went viral, the fame would have come to us.

Oh, well.

We stood and chitchatted awhile longer, but then it was time to go. We said our good-byes and started to leave. I was proud of Hambone. And I was about to tell him this when all of a sudden, a handful of dirt smacked him right in the face–thwap!

The gorilla responsible started jumping up and down, laughing hysterically.

I looked at Hambone.

Boy, was he mad.

Don't do it, I told him. Don't do what I know you're going to do. Be better than that. Be a bigger dog.

But do you think he listened to me?

Of course not.

But that's a story for another time...

Peas and Hambone's
guide to:
Movies We Know By Heart

Gone With the Trash (p. 15)
During the Civil War, puppies Brett and Violet struggle with recycling. Brett refuses to sort his cardboard. Will Violet still find him adorable?

The Wizard of Paws (p. 36)
When a cyclone tears through Tigertown it carries Eliza and her dog Bobo to the magical land called Paws. How will they get back home?

Johnny Maloney (p. 47)
Johnny, a down-on-his-luck sports agent tries to get his football playing dog a million dollar contract. Show me the Milk-Bones!

Bite Club (p. 71)
Searching for the meaning of life, a pack of stray dogs form a club and bite each other.

The Wolfpack (p. 73)
A band of wolves gets separated from the pack and has to fight there way back home to Boney Island.

CLAWS (p. 83)

When a man-eating lion begins to menace the small community of Hamity, an animal control officer, a zookeeper, and a grizzled old lion tamer set out to stop it.

BRAVETAIL (p. 98)

Based on a true story, the legendary Scottish Terrier known as William Waggish rallies a group of stray dogs against an English Bull Terrier who rules the neighborhood with an iron fist.

APAWCALYPSE NOW (p. III)

Soldier dog WIlly must journey deep into the jungles of Vietnam to retrieve wayward officer Colonel Furtz.

ALL ABOUT AKITA (p. 140)

Aspiring actress Akita Hairylegs lies and cheats her way to becoming the biggest star since Rin Tin Tin.

DIRTY HAIRY (p. 163)

K-9 officer Hairy Chihuahua tries to track down a crazy Poweranian who has dognapped prized poodle Mrs. Poofball.

A FIELD OF THEIR OWN (p. 169)

Two sisters join the first female professional fetch league and by the end of the season are competing for the championship.

Cool Hand Duke (p. 179)

Duke Hacksaw, a Pug who doesn't play by the rules, refuses to roll over in a Southern dog pound.

Goodfidos (p. 188)

The story of Henry Hound, part Irish Wolfhound and part Italian Greyhound and how he attempts to climb his way to the top of a gang of purebreds.

Midnight Cowdog (p. 192)

A naïve cowdog travels to New York City to seek fame and fortune and in the process discovers all he really needs is a friend.

Airkennel (p. 208)

Former pilot Red Striker never thought he'd get back in the cockpit again but when the passengers and crew become ill he's the only dog who can land the kennel safely.

In the Beef of the Night (p. 221)

Pet detective Smokey Ribbs joins forces with dog hating poice chief Buddy Lungapoo to track down the person responsible for stealing 100 pounds of kibble.

Planet of the Cats (p. 225)

A crew of canine astronauts crash-lands on a planet where intelligent talking cats are the dominant species and dogs are kept in cages.

Canine Network (p. 241)

Fed up newshound Howard Beagle becomes a celebrity after howling against the dog-eat-dog world he lives in.

Monty Poodle and the Howly Trail (p. 249)

King Charles Spaniel and his pack travel the countryside to find the Trail, meeting strange animals along the way.

Goatbusters (p. 250)

Four sheepdogs go into business to rid the countryside of paranormal goats.

ATTACK OF THE ZOMBIE GORILLAS!

OH-MY-_gosh_! Zombie gorillas are attacking!
     silly word

First thing you have to do is take a _belly_ breath.
                               adjective

Good. Now, grab an ax and a pick shovel. Don't

have one handy? Don't fear. You can use a

sord , a couple of _lasy rs_ ,
  noun   something alive (plural)

and lots of _petza_. Watch out! There's one
          food

right behind you! Boy, that's one _big_ zombie
                               adjective

gorilla. It looks positively _groing_ . Better run. Oh,
                        adjective

274

no. You're getting _tired_. You have to rest. No.
adjective

You have to hide behind that _car_. Coast is
adjective

clear. But wait a second. What's that noise? Sounds

like a _footstep_. OH-MY _gosh_! It's a zombie
noun   silly word

gorilla. It found you. It _screamed_. Then it growls.
verb

Kind of like it's saying, "I want to _eat_
verb

your _bread_ off." You scream. Then you _faint_.
body part   verb

When you wake up you realize you're locked

in a _dongth_ Luckily, there's a key under the
noun

275

_rug___ . You open the door and run as _quicly_
noun   -ly ending word

as you can. When you get to your _House_ , you
                                    noun

tell your mom and dad what happened. They don't

believe you. They think you are _crazy_. So
                                  adjective

they call _dr.oz___ and _dr.molly_ .
          celebrity (male)   celebrity (female)

You have to go and see them first thing in the

morning. _wow_, you think. I wish that zombie
          Exclamation

gorilla had eaten my _head_ off, instead.
                      body part

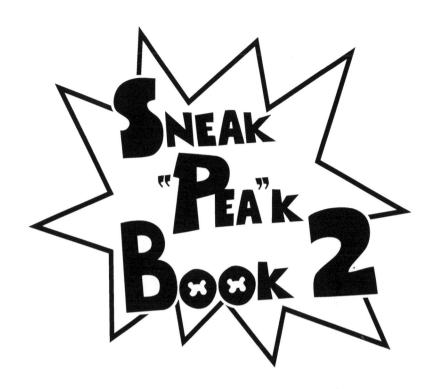

PEAS AND HAMBONE:

SAVE THEMSELVES!

Gulp!

I start counting. One. Two. Three. Four...
ah, forget it. There's too many of them to
count.

What are we going to do?

Sorry.

Kind of jumped right into the middle of
the action on you.

Well, here's what you need to know:

Hambone puts his paws on my
shoulders. "On the count of three we go," he
says.

"Just like that?"

"Just like that—ready?"

I take a deep breath. "As ready as I'll
ever be."

"One...two..." Hambone unlocks the

sliding glass door and runs out. "Banzaiiiiii!"

"What happened to three?" I say, running behind him.

"Look at that," says Hambone. "He's running away like a scaredy cat."

And it's true. The moment he sees us coming out the sliding glass door, Evil Doctor Crazy Gorilla drops the bottles and hightails it off the porch. He's now running for my dad's shed.

Hambone stops and points. "Scaredy cat, scaredy cat," he says.

"Um...Hambone," I say.

"Scaredy cat. Scaredy cat."

I tap him on the shoulder. "Um... Hambone...you might want to focus over here. We have kind of a situation developing."

And what a situation it is: thermoplastic Evil Doctor Crazy Gorillas swarming all around us.

One. Two. Three. Four… ah, forget it. There's too many of them to count.

How are we ever going to get out of this one???

COLOR YOUR OWN
Evil Laboratory!

About the Author

When Todd Nichols was eight years old, he asked, no, he pleaded, no, he begged his parents to get him a dog. They said no. Not a chance. Never going to happen. Not even when pigs started to fly. So he had to settle for the next best thing. Which was writing stories about a boy and his dog. When Todd's not coming up with more awesome Peas and Hambone adventures he loves collecting rocks, eating pizza, and catching pennies off his elbow.

About the Illustrator

When Chris was eight years old, he dreamed of becoming a professional matchbox car racer. In his free time he doodles endlessly and makes things.

71368954R00161

Made in the USA
Middletown, DE
23 April 2018